SEAL Undercover

By

Desiree Holt
USA Today and Amazon
Bestselling author
and
Suspense Sisters

Silver SEALs Series

SEAL Undercover

Copyright 2019 by Desiree Holt

Published by Desiree Holt

Cover Art by Becky McGraw

Beta Reader: Margie Hager

Editor: Kate Richards

To

former SEAL Jack Carr

An incredible individual

Thank you for all your help and invaluable information

This book could not have been written without you.

You are the embodiment of what this country stands for

And the heroes we all hold in high esteem.

And to all SEALs everywhere, past, current and future

Thank you for your service.

Acknowledgments

This book, as always, is the result of the effort of so many people. First and foremost, Margie Hager, my wonderful beta reader who has been with me forever. Kate Richards, editor par excellence, who whips my manuscripts into shape with expertise. My Virtual Assistant, Maria Connor, without whom nothing would happen. Joe Trainor, prior military and current law enforcement resource who answers endless questions and is an incredible source of information. Last but far from least, my son Steven Horwitz who handles all the business and marketing details so incredibly well.

Thank you, all of you, for your excellent help.

Dear Readers,

Writing a book is a labor of love for me. My characters take over my life, and I work to make them come alive for all of you. I hope each effort pleases you and results in an enjoyable story. That's because without you, my wonderful readers, there would be no Desiree Holt. You enrich my life and inspire me and I love you all.

You can always reach me at authordesireeholt@gmail.com, and I invite you to join my reader group, where there is always something happening.
https://www.facebook.com/groups/DesireeHoltReaderGroup/?epa=SEARCH_BOX

Looking forward to "seeing" you there.

Desiree

Where else can you find me:

www.facebook.com/desireeholtauthor

www.facebook.com/desiree01holt

Twitter @desireeholt

Pinterest: desiree02holt

Google: https://g.co/kgs/6vgLUu

www.desireeholt.com www.desiremeonly.com

Follow me on BookBub

https://www.bookbub.com/search?search=Desiree+Holt

Amazon https://www.amazon.com/Desiree-Holt/e/B003LD2Q3M/ref=sr_tc_2_0?qid=1505488204&sr=1-2-ent

https://bookandmainbites.com/users/20900

Signup for my newsletter and receive a free book:

Sswww.desireeholt.com/newsletter

Max DiSalvo gave his entire life to the SEALs. He would have married—he certainly enjoyed women—but he never could find one who understood his dedication to the Teams, even though many of his team members married happily. It takes a certain caliber of woman to be a SEAL wife, and Max just never found one who fit with him. Now, at forty-eight, he is out of the SEALs, running his own commercial fishing company in Maine where he grew up, and waiting for his assignments from DHS.

Regan Shaw, a SEAL widow, is an Intelligence Operations Specialist with DHS, and a woman who Max is drawn to from first sight. Part of her job is analyzing information to assess threats, and she's discovered a doozy—there is a secret group of very wealthy people who, in partnership with a powerful cartel, are using the border with Mexico to smuggle terrorists from the Middle East into the country. Word has leaked that the cabal is planning a terrorist attack to take over the country on a national holiday, and a high-level member of the government is clearing the way with them for everything.

The group is about to have one of its executive meetings at an exclusive resort in Texas and that's where Bone Frog Command is sending Max and Regan as husband and wife. Credentials have been arranged, and a story has been set, and there is backup for him should he need it, but the orders are: get in, get the information, and get out.

It doesn't take long for them to realize how dangerous this group is and that it must be stopped. Now. When someone betrays them, and Regan is kidnapped, Max goes into war mode because, in Regan Shaw, he's found the woman he's waited for all his life, and he doesn't intend to lose her now. But he will need every bit of the skills he learned as a SEAL to rescue her and bring down this very dirty conspiracy.

Prologue

"This is just fucking bullshit." Gavin Emery leaned forward in his chair, his face set in angry lines. His hoarse growl caught everyone's attention. "How do we know this is even real?"

Jed Whitlow looked at the hologram in front of him. "Because I say so, and there's no fucking way I'd lie to you or anyone else in this group. We've been together too long, and the plan is too critical, especially at this point. We are almost at the target date."

Jed was the one who had called the meeting so suddenly that the only option was to hold it holographically. They all lived too far away from each other to hold it live. At least this way they'd all be able to see each other. The eight people gathered for this represented a major portion of the wealth in North America and wielded significant behind-the-scenes power, globally as well as nationally. In two weeks, they would gather at the Whitlows' hunting lodge—although the luxury of the place made it too extravagant to call a lodge. The subject of the meeting was the critical last step in a complex plan they had been working on for three years. They were much too far into it to pull the plug, so this news made them all tense and on edge.

"Okay then, Jed. You're up," Gavin told him. "You're the one who got the call and went to see Bernardo. Are we in a bunch of shit here?"

"I don't think so." Jed cleared his throat. "First of all, let me remind you that Bernardo and I have known each other since college. Even though he lives in Colorado. We've kept in touch over the years, and I knew this was something he'd buy into 100 percent. He's been a valuable asset from Day One, as has his wife, Jeanne. Her skill at plucking information out of thin air has helped Ferren Arms and Munitions Manufacturing to grow to the size it is now."

"But your message told us the situation has changed," Emery pointed out.

"It has." Jed paused. "As you all know, three days ago, at ten fifteen in the morning, Bernardo suffered a major heart attack. Luckily, he was home. His wife called EMS, and he was rushed to the hospital, where he's still in the cardiac care unit. I flew up to see him at once, and it seems his recovery won't be happening anytime soon. He may even need open-heart surgery." He paused. "Questions so far?"

"Where do we stand now?" Emery persisted. "You say he's out, which could be a fucking disaster. He's the one providing all the supplies we need for this as well as the means to deliver them."

Lorena Alvaro leaned forward in her chair. Jed noticed that even at this early hour she was perfectly put together, as if attending the meeting in person. Her vanity and obsession with not showing her age were legendary, and she hadn't yet figured out that none of them gave a flying fuck what she looked like as long as she did her part.

"Yes. How can we be sure this isn't being faked? Maybe he just got cold feet now that we're down to the wire and at the last minute wanted out. Leaving us in a terrible position, I might add. Are we even sure this is a real episode? I've had a doubt or two about him of late."

Jed ground his teeth. This woman got on his nerves, and things like that could throw a monkey wrench into their plans.

"He's done absolutely nothing to make you feel that way." He might have said the words with a little more force than necessary. "As I said earlier, I've known him for years, and that's just not in his wheelhouse. That's why I felt confident reaching out to him at the start. You don't flourish in the arms business if it is. He's more upset about this than we are. His doctors are having to increase his medication because of that to make sure he doesn't have another attack."

"You're sure?" Lorena persisted.

Why couldn't she just take his word for it so they could get on with the business at hand? If it weren't for the fact she and her contacts were such a critical piece of this operation, he'd uninvite her.

"You don't have open-heart surgery scheduled just to miss a meeting, Lorena. I spoke at length to both his doctor and his wife when I was there and, I can assure you, this is real."

"Just remember," Lorena pointed out, "that this plan came about because of Elias and myself. We were the ones originally being paid to let the cartel use our land to get their drugs into this country."

"And collected even more when they told you they wanted to up the ante and smuggle high-value terrorists in along with those drugs," Kurt Cavanaugh pointed out.

"They were already getting paid a king's ransom to do it, so there was plenty to share," Gavin added. "But few of their 'clients' had any idea of what they would do next except to wage small attacks on multiple areas of this country. Kill a lot of people. Those people have no idea how much 'a lot' really is."

"Yes, well, without that we'd never be able to put this plan in place," Lorena pointed out, "so pardon me if I'm a little edgy about this change in the situation. You would all do well to remember that. Now, tell me." Lorena crossed her legs. "How is Jeanne taking it? I always saw her as a weak link. Maybe we need to handle her until this is over."

Jed wanted to smash something. Why did Lorena always have to be such a bitch? Her "handling" of things always resulted in bloodshed.

"She's upset, as you can imagine," he answered, "but holding it together. And she's not a weak link, as you put it, Lorena. She knows what's at stake here, just as everyone does. But obviously, if he's not coming to the meeting, neither is she."

"Of course," Lorena snapped.

They had all met originally and formed their little group as couples. Although each marriage had a dominant partner, they had all been equals at the table, each an integral part of the group. Each of them brought a vital contribution to the organization and was as committed to The Plan as their spouse. Now the unspoken question that hovered in the air was who would replace the Ferrens and make sure their contribution didn't disappear?

Jeanne Ferren was a specialist at analyzing data, something she'd learned working for a defense contractor long before she and Bernardo had married and with great care built their place at the top level of society. She'd had no problem at all turning that knowledge to helping them with their overall long-term project. Bernardo, a manufacturer and world-wide distributor of arms and munitions, knew exactly what to use and where and when to use it. He would also supply all the weapons for the schedule of "events" in the timeline.

"There can't be any places at the table vacant now," Gavin pointed out. "The last two pieces of the puzzle will be arriving this week. This meeting coming up is to put the finishing touches on the plans and be ready to move forward." He shook his head. "This is a terrible time for him to have a heart attack."

"I'll be sure to pass that along to him." Jed's voice was edged with sarcasm.

"So, tell us. Just who is going to replace them? We can't recruit strangers at this point. And what about the arms he's providing? That's a fucking lot of firearms and munitions to try and get somewhere at the last minute, even if we could find someone to trust." Kurt glared at the holographic images, his stare biting into those viewing the meeting. "We have spent months—no, years—planning, and we are too far into this to call it off. We will never have another chance like this. Everyone—and I mean *everyone*—is ready to move forward once these next players arrive. We can't drop just anyone into this. If it weren't for the arms and munitions that are at the heart of this, I'd say just move forward."

Jed personally thought it was a stroke of luck Bernardo had a good solution for them, but he wasn't sure if everyone else would think so. Max Ferren, Bernardo's brother, was his partner in the company and knew exactly what was going on. Was he as plugged in to the operation as Bernardo was? The man had assured him that was the case.

What about his wife, though? Did she have the same skills as her sister-in-law? He wished he'd been able to meet them when he was there, but they were just at that moment returning from a trip out of state. Fuck it all to hell, anyway. This group had planned so carefully and worked so hard to kick off their plan with a bang—literally—choosing the target date for maximum impact. They could not afford a screwup now.

He cleared his throat.

"Bernardo has an answer to the problem," Jed told them. "I wanted to double-check everything before I brought it to you, but this is as perfect as it can get. Bernardo's brother, Max, will take his place. Max is Bernardo's partner in Ferren Arms Manufacturing and has been involved in a number of activities they've 'sponsored.' You know the two men are very close ideologically and share many of the same contacts, or Bernardo would never have been able to commit to this plan. To be a part of it. He promises we can trust his brother as we do him, and I believe him."

"Bring a stranger in?" Kurt snapped. "I don't care who he is. I'm not sure I'd feel comfortable with that."

"Well, we can't leave those seats vacant," Jed snapped. "Max is hardly a stranger, and we need the weapons. Did you want to buy them on the open market?"

There was a long moment of silence.

"I've met Max, and I trust him," Jed added in a slow voice. "He and Bernardo are tight as brothers as well as partners. He wouldn't recommend the man, brother or not, unless he was confident he could step right in. We knew from the beginning that Bernardo shared everything with him. A damn good thing, too, since he's now fully briefed and ready to assume a seat at the table. The last thing Bernardo would do, especially at this point, is send in someone who could fuck everything up and put us all at great risk." He paused. "Including himself, I might add. Anyway, I met Max a couple of times over the years, and I can assure you he's got his shit together every bit as much as Bernardo does."

"I guess we'll just have to take your word for it, Jed." Lorena glared at him through the hologram. "Besides, we're past the stopping point, and we need the Ferren supplies. We'll just have to put Max Ferren—and his wife, don't forget—under a magnifying glass. Do we have pictures of them?"

Jed nodded. "I'll be sending them along as soon as I hang up. I'll also forward every bit of information on them. I started a search just before this phone call."

"And Bernardo? How does he feel about being left out of the action?" Gavin Emery glared at the other images.

"He's upset, naturally. He's funded revolutions in other countries for financial gain, and he badly wanted an active part in this one." Jed sighed. "Truthfully, however, I think having to deal with all this may have been one cause of the heart attack. His health hasn't been all that good. I think he's been hanging on until everything was in place and we could assume control. Of everything."

"How well protected is he in the hospital?" Lorena asked. "No media or anyone can get to him?"

Jed nodded. "He's hired top-level security. No one will get through those men."

Everyone was silent for a long moment.

Finally Gavin cleared his throat. "I'm not happy with this, but we don't have a choice. We're too far into this to call it off now. And we all agreed July 4th was ideal for this, symbolic as it is."

Everyone nodded their agreement.

"When do we meet this perfect substitute?" Lorena asked, a nasty edge to her voice.

"He and his wife will be here next week. They'll be staying at my hotel in town for a couple of days so I can meet with them and vet them, just to be sure. They shouldn't be anywhere near the lodge until I'm satisfied he's not a plant."

"A plant?" Lorena's words had a sharp edge. "Who would plant someone in our group? How would they even find out about us? We've gone overboard with the secrecy on this." She paused. "Right? Everyone agree to that?"

Each of them murmured their agreement.

"So how do we think something like that can happen? If anyone in this group has been flapping their lips, I will shoot you myself."

"Lorena, no one's been talking out of school," Jed soothed. "We all have too much at stake to do that."

"What about Max Ferren's wife?" Gavin asked. "Has she been read in? And what does she bring to the table?"

Jed nodded. "She's been included since the beginning, just like Max." He smiled. "And she brings skills to those her sister-in-law has. As I said earlier, she knows how to hack into secure systems and analyze data."

"So she'd be able to let us know if any word of our plan leaked out?" Gavin's smile was more vicious than friendly. "Good."

"I'm meeting them at the hotel next Tuesday. That will give me two days to turn him upside down before we all arrive at the lodge."

"And that's exactly what you'll be doing," Gavin stated. "We're too close to our goal for anything to go wrong."

"I'll keep you all in the loop."

"Be sure you do that," Kurt growled.

Jed shut down the video conference and sat back in his chair. Bernardo was his oldest friend. He trusted him completely. He just wished he didn't have this little feeling of unease running through him. He hated last-minute change. It always screwed something up. If it happened here, it could blow up in their faces.

Literally.

Chapter One

Max DiSalvo (Commander, Navy SEALs Ret) double-checked to make sure his boat, the lead boat in his small fleet, was securely moored in its slip before heading along the dock. Next he made sure that everything was locked up in the small shed where he kept extra equipment and where they finished cleaning at the end of the day. Finally he climbed the steps to the parking lot where his truck sat. His shoulder still bothered him now and then, but it didn't keep him from pulling his share of the load. It just meant a hot shower at the end of the day and an application of the stuff the therapist had given him. He'd learned to live with the twinges and the stiffness when the weather was really cold. He was grateful that it hadn't been worse, even if it had ended his career as an active duty SEAL.

Hauling himself into the driver's seat, he rolled down his window and sat for a moment before cranking the ignition, just enjoying the scene. The sun was setting, its rays warming the air and sending heat through the windshield. The scent of sea salt filled the air, mingled with the aroma of fresh fish and diesel fuel. Another good day on the water. His crew had packed the entire catch up for delivery and taken off, so all he had to do was— What? Shower and change? Have a cup of coffee? A drink? Was that what his life had come to?

As a teenager, he had loved working in his family's small but productive fishing company. He'd also spent summers at it until he graduated from college. He loved being on the water and, when he wasn't working a boat crew, he was swimming, kayaking, or enjoying other water sports with his friends. Was it any wonder he ended up being a SEAL?

Once he joined the Navy and was accepted into the SEALs, he'd had no more time for the company. If he wasn't on a mission, he was training for it or involved in rugged activities with his fellow SEALs. And enjoying women. Nothing serious. He was married to the SEALs. But he did enjoy the ones he spent time with. He figured when he settled down, so to speak, he'd have plenty of time to concentrate on a woman.

That moment in his life came sooner than he expected. At forty-eight he hadn't been quite ready to leave the SEALs, but he didn't have a choice. On the final mission he led his SEAL team, he'd been shot twice in his shoulder, the bullet seriously impacting the muscle and bone structure. The injury had ended his career as an active duty SEAL, and that had been the bitterest pill. He had done his best to requalify, sweating through all the therapy sessions and repeating the exercises at home, forcing himself through the pain to practice on the gun range, but it hadn't been enough. His attempt to be restored to active duty had been an epic failure, one he had to get over if he was going to enjoy the rest of his life.

So now here he was, Commander Max DiSalvo, Retired, trying to step back into a life he hadn't known for years and wondering if he'd be able to do it. Or even wanted to. He still had the skills, no question about that. Some things you never forgot. He was still physically fit, even allowing for the shoulder. So what if he had more gray hair on his head than he'd like. Maybe it made him look distinguished. And he couldn't deny that commercial fishing gave him a sense of peace he hadn't known for a very long time.

On the way home to Maine, he'd turned his thoughts to the future that had a remarkably different outlook. His parents, now in their late seventies, had been hinting about retiring and indulging their passion for traveling. Max had often thought about spending his days working on the ocean he loved so much, running the fishing boats he'd grown up on. He just hadn't expected it to happen so soon. At least, he thought, he had a plan, a purpose for after the SEALs, which so many men he knew did not.

A few strokes of a pen had turned the company over to him. It was like putting on an old familiar sweater, and he had to admit he loved it. The fishing. Watching the sunsets. Being on the water. Reconnecting with some old friends.

Today had been great, catchwise. He had a top-quality crew and top-notch captains for the other three boats, but his life had holes in it. Perhaps he'd left attention to the personal part too long. Maybe that was why he couldn't get rid of this restless feeling.

Shaking his head, he started the engine, pulled out of the lot, and headed for home. These days, that was a small New England colonial with a wide front porch. He'd thought of renting, but Sunset Harbor, as small as it was, only had two rental complexes, and neither one really appealed to him.

What if she doesn't like it?

He had no fucking idea who *she* was, or how or when he'd even meet a *she*. He obviously hadn't prepared well on that front. Just dragged his sorry ass back to Sunset Harbor, took over the reins of DiSalvo Commercial Fishing, plunked down a deposit on the house, and somehow expected his life to suddenly come together. The first six months he'd been busy getting reacclimated to civilian life, to his small hometown, and reconnecting with some of the people he'd known years before. As long as his right hand held up, he hadn't missed female companionship.

But he felt it was time to make some changes in his life in that direction. Now that he had a stable, settled life, he didn't want to live it alone. Not that he'd made a real effort to find female companionship. But he was growing tired of moving from one day to the next and wondering if this was a sad forecast of the rest of his future.

With a sigh, he showered off the fish smell and pulled on clean jeans and a DiSalvo T-shirt, checked the dismal contents of the fridge, and decided he'd have dinner and a beer at The Rusty Scupper. Ted Doyle always served the best food, didn't pester him with questions, and he could hang out or not.

Less than thirty minutes later, he was situated on a stool at the polished oak bar at the Scupper, sipping on a local craft beer and waiting for his meatloaf and mashed potatoes. A not very glamourous meal, but damn! Nobody made it better than Ted's cook. Maybe when he found a woman that would be one of the requirements. But first he had to start looking, and Sunset Harbor had a woefully short list of candidates.

"Here you go." Ted slid the plate onto the counter in front of him, the fragrance of the food drifting up in a cloud of steam.

"Man, if your cook was single, I might have to marry him," he joked.

"Maybe you can catch him on one of the nights his wife kicks him out of the house. Enjoy."

He was just swallowing the last bite of his dinner and working his way through his second beer when a hand clapped down on his shoulder. At first, he tensed, wondering who was touching him that way. But when he turned his head, he found himself smiling.

"Crash? Holy shit, is that you? Si, it's good to see you." He looked the man up and down. "But what the hell kind of costume party you dressed up for?"

Navy SEAL Silas "Si" Branson would always be Crash to his SEAL friends, the reminder of his famous joyriding episode. The man was tall as ever and still looking fit. Only, instead of fatigues or jeans, he was decked out in a tailored navy suit with a white shirt and a striped tie. His hair was cut a lot shorter, too, and when Max looked down, he saw Si's feet were shod in what looked like expensive loafers.

"If only." His friend sighed.

"So I guess the rumors are true. You've gone over to the dark side."

"It's a lot darker than you think," Si grunted. "So, how's the shoulder? Heard it might be kind of gimpy."

Anger rose up in Max at the mention of his injury. It had ruined his career as a SEAL, and talking about it made him want to throw something. Or hit someone.

"Doesn't hurt my fishing," he snapped.

"Hey, hey, hey." Si held his hands up, palms outward. "Just asking. I have the same kind of problem. Wrecked my back and just could not come back from it. Killed me with the SEALS."

Max was instantly contrite. "Sorry to hear that, buddy. And sorry I bit your head off."

Si shrugged. "No biggie. I know just how you feel. So, no women in your life these days? I thought for sure the minute you retired you'd have a long string of them."

Max's laugh was short and sharp. "Yeah, I might have to look beyond Sunset Harbor for that. Seems the best women here are already taken. Anyway, how's

Maggie? Did I hear right that the two of you kissed and made up and got hitched again?"

"You did." Si had a proud look on his face. "And she's due to pop any day now."

Max's jaw dropped. "She's pregnant? Well, good for you guys."

Everyone in their tight-knit SEAL circle knew about the death of Si and Maggie's son, the emotional devastation that followed, and the divorce. He was glad for his friend and wondered for a moment if he'd ever have that kind of emotional commitment with anyone.

Shut up. Si's not here so you can complain about your love life. Or lack of it.

"As a matter of fact," Si continued, "she's one of the main reasons I have this new job."

"Oh yeah?" Max lifted an eyebrow. "How's that?"

"Her connections got me the interview and it was all the way after that." Si nodded at Max's plate. "If you're through with your meal, let's head to that booth in the corner and I'll tell you."

"Oh? We need privacy for this?" Max could not imagine why that was. Except... Wait a minute. Hadn't he heard through the SEALs' grapevine that Si was now with the Department of Homeland Security?

"For sure."

"Okay. How about a beer? Or coffee? Something to wet your throat while we talk."

"Coffee would be great." Si grimaced. "It's been a long day."

As soon as they were settled in the booth, Max looked at his friend. "So, tell me about this cushy office job you have now."

Si barked a laugh. "I'm not in the office that much and I'd hardly call it cushy. But it's the reason I'm here."

"And that is?" Max kept his voice even.

Si reached into his inside beast pocket, pulled out a photo, and slapped it on the table.

Max's eyebrows shot up nearly to his hairline.

"Is that a picture of me? Where the hell did you get it, and what are you doing with it? And how did my face get in a picture at an event I've never attended?" He stared at the photograph. "Wait. There's something different... Hell! That's not me, but I sure as hell could pass for him."

"Exactly. He also happens to be named Max. Max Ferren."

Max DiSalvo frowned. "Do I know him?"

"No. He and his brother, Bernardo, have made

billions in the arms and munitions industry."

"Yeah? Why does that give me a bad feeling?"

"Because you always were a smart son of a bitch, with good instincts."

Max was still looking at the photo. "So, what is it you want from me?"

"How would you like to go to a very private, very small meeting with people who want to take over this country?"

Max was sure his jaw dropped far enough to hit the table.

"Are you shitting me?"

Si shook his head. "Not even a little. Look. I head up a unit of the DHS that's so secret no one ever mentions it. We deal with the threats to national security that are so heavy, one misstep and the country goes to hell. We have a dangerous situation evolving here, Max, and I need you. Your country needs you. It's not done with you yet. If you're up for it, we need to go someplace more private to talk." He paused. "And then, if you're in, we need to head to the D.C. area."

It took Max all of three seconds to make up his mind. He jogged over to the bar, slapped some bills on it then motioned to Si to head out the door with him.

"Where's your car?" he asked. When Si pointed, Max said, "Follow me."

Fifteen minutes later, they were in Max's living room, Max sitting and Si pacing.

"First of all," Si began, "I have this super-secret group within the DHS. It was my idea, and the director supports it. A small number of retired SEAL officers who can lead a group of multi-agency operatives when needed on missions no one else can know about."

"And what's this group of yours called?"

Si grinned. "The Bone Frog Command."

Max chuckled. "I couldn't have picked a better one."

Every SEAL knew that in the Vietnam era Navy SEALs were known as frogmen. In the early 2000s, a new image for the SEAL Teams began to emerge, a skeleton of a frog that paid homage to those earlier generations of SEALs. It became the inspiration for tattoos on many SEAL Team warriors. Max had one as did several of his SEAL friends.

"So," he prodded, "what is it you want from me?"

"I want you to go to this meeting where there's a good chance someone will try to kill you, get all the information you can, and get out with your skin intact so we can destroy this before it gets off the ground.

And lock these people away."

"That's all?" Max burst out laughing. "You make it sound so appealing." Then he looked at Si's face and all laughter went away. "You're serious. Okay. Let's have it. What's this all about?"

Si cleared his throat. "There is a group—a cabal— of five couples who live in some of the Western states. They control enormous wealth and have vast, silent, almost invisible reaches of power. They think they are untouchable gods who can do anything they want."

"And what is it they want?"

"More power. All the power. Like I said earlier, their goal is to gain full control of the United States. To get rid of the government as we know it and have every bit of power in their hands, with their own puppet at the head so they can pull the strings."

Max whistled. "Holy shit."

"Yeah. No kidding. There's some kickers here." He ticked them off on his fingers. "One. They want to get rid of everyone in key positions of power and replace them with their own people. Two. They've been in bed with one of the most powerful cartels for some time. The Rojas cartel. One of them had the original connection and was providing a safe passage the cartel could use to bring drugs into this country. Apparently, along the way, the cartel added terrorists looking for new, fertile territory to rebuild their power. Now these people are working with that cartel to smuggle some of the worst, most high-value extremists over the border into this country."

Max could feel the color draining from his face. "God. For what purpose?"

"Like I said, they have delusions of grandeur and want to take over this country. The chatter we've captured indicates their first step is a massive terror strike to dismantle the government. The unholy thought at Bone Frog is that the cabal has made a deal with these terrorists to be group leaders, with small armies made up of low-level terrorists and cartel soldiers."

For a moment, Max was afraid he would throw up.

"Terrorism is, as we know, a tactic. A strategy used to achieve a specific end. One effect of what they're planning is the weakening of the American economy by forcing massive spending on security. But that's only stage two. Others will follow as the country collapses and these maniacs take control."

Max dipped his head. "Go on."

"The cabal is pandering to the desires of these animals," Si continued, "to help create a network in this country as they've done in their own. Then these traitors can destroy our existing structure through fear and intimidation and take over the country. With, we assume, the cartel soldiers as backup enforcement. That gives them an open market for their drugs with no controls." He paused. "Think of it, Max. Their plan is to control the government, the media, the schools, the military. You name it."

"Jesus Christ, Si." Max could feel the blood draining from his face. He'd fought enough years in the sandbox to know what kind of governments operated when people like this were in charge.

"No kidding. And that's not all. One of the three top people in the government is their new chosen figurehead. Someone who already has incredible power. He—or she, I guess—is helping them with this."

Max stared at him. "The president?"

Si shrugged. "That's one possibility. But it's definitely at that level. We need you to find out who that person is and, so far, we're stymied."

"You know," Max said slowly, "this sounds like they want to take over the world where others using the same methods have failed."

"I wouldn't say no to that. It's what terrifies us. And we have a very short time frame."

"What do you mean?"

"According to the chatter we've picked up, the big launch is scheduled for three weeks from now." He paused. "July 4th."

Max wanted to believe he'd heard wrong but knew he hadn't. Holy motherfucker. He pushed himself out of his chair and went to stare out the big window, hands in his pockets, brain rushing full steam ahead.

"They picked Independence Day to take away the country's independence?"

"That's exactly what the fuckers did." Si spat out the words. "That's why we need you to help us stop them."

"And just how am I supposed to do this? Exactly?"

"That picture I showed you of the guy who could be your doppelganger?"

Max nodded.

"He's suddenly become a key player."

"Suddenly?" Max frowned. "You'd better explain that."

"Okay. DHS has been working on this for two years, ever since they got the first hint of trouble. Once we knew all the names involved, we dug around looking for anything that gave us some leverage. We got one lucky break. We got information on Bernardo

Ferren, arms and munitions billionaire, of some things he's done that could send him to prison for a long time. Illegal arms sales. Hiding money in offshore accounts. Funding revolutions in small countries to provide more markets for his merchandise."

Max made a rude noise. "Nice guy."

"Tell me about it." A muscle ticked in his jaw, the only sign of the stress he was under. "We were only able to learn the date this thing explodes a couple of days ago. And think about it, Max. We can't even alert the military without sending signals to everyone and his brother. Not to mention the fact, where would we send them? There are so many logical targets, I'm not even sure we have enough military to cover them all."

"Fuck." It was all Max could think of to say. He was well aware of the effect multiple terrorists strikes would have in this country.

"Anyway," Si continued, "we don't have too many options. We need confirmation of the date and a blueprint of the strikes. We 'convinced' Bernardo to have a heart attack and to tell the others his brother, Max, will be taking his place." He paused. "The man you're a dead ringer for. And who, by the way, as you're now aware, coincidentally happens to have the same first name you do."

Max snorted. "I hope you aren't using the word 'dead' literally."

One corner of Si's mouth turned up in a half grin. "Only figuratively, I promise you."

"Do the others in this disgusting group know they're getting a substitute? Are they even willing to do this?"

"Jed Whitlow, the person who put this group together, made sure everyone knew this was their best and only course of action. Bernardo, at our urging, was very convincing."

"I won't even ask what you mean by urging. But let me ask you this. What makes you think Bernardo won't spill the beans? Or get away from his hospital room?"

Si's smile was positively evil. "Because we have four former SEALs guarding him day and night. Jed Whitlow, who flew up to see him, thinks they are private security Ferren has hired. When he came to check it out, we made sure everyone, including Ferren, put on a good performance."

"And what does he get out of it?"

"He thinks he's getting a free pass on prison and will have the opportunity to live out his life on some island in luxury."

"He thinks? And what's really going to happen."

"That's above my pay grade." He walked over to Max. "Anyway, as soon as I saw the picture and heard the name, I knew we had to get you into this. You've got all the necessary skills. If you say yes, you've got five days to learn everything you need to know to become Max Ferren."

"What happens then?"

"Their next very private, very secret meeting I told you about? It's taking place at a lodge hidden away from the world. We believe it's the final get-together before July 4th. We want you to go in there as Max Ferren and get every bit of information available to bring them down."

Max gave a hard laugh. "You don't want much, do you."

"Listen. You're our only chance. There's no one else we can insert. We'll give you all the protection we can. But, in the end, it may be up to you." He sighed. "Will you do it, Max? I know this is a cheesy line, but like I said earlier, your country needs you."

Max stared out the window for a long time. He knew this was risky. He might even get killed. But for the first time since he'd been shot, his blood was stirring and his pulse racing. He had a purpose. This was what he lived for. To serve his country in any way he could.

"Well?" Si prodded.

Max turned. "You knew I'd do it, or you'd never have come here. But I need the morning to get things organized with the boat crews and put someone in charge while I'm away."

"No problem."

"Fourth of July, huh? They picked a symbolic day to do this. On purpose, I'm sure."

"No shit. The assholes. I'd like to take them apart myself." He paused. "There's one more thing. I haven't discussed it with anyone except my boss and Regan."

"Yeah? What's that?"

"Part of their attack could include biological weapons."

Max's blood chilled, and he had trouble breathing. "Bioterrorism? Are you kidding me?"

"I hope so. We haven't picked up any chatter about it, but you know it is a favorite of the terrorists in the Middle East."

Max knew that very well. The possibility of it on missions was always there in the background, which was why they carried special gear.

"Fuck, Si. We need to shut this damn thing down

before it goes any further."

Si nodded. "That we do. Okay, I'll have the chopper pick us up at one tomorrow. That do it for you?"

"The chopper?" Max chuckled. "Yeah, that'll be fine, but we'd better do it somewhere away from here, or the townspeople will be gossiping twenty-four seven."

"Gotcha. Oh, and there's a bonus with this. You'll have a wife with you."

"A wife?" Max stared at his friend.

"Yeah. Max Ferren was recently married. No one in the group has met her, but we had Bernardo vouch for her along with his brother."

"They can't be too happy about all this."

Si nodded. "They're not. But Bernardo's been a driving force in this group. His arms and munitions are the key to pulling this off. He's had to reach out to others to gather the quantity he needs, which means they're no doubt already setting up the beginning of their worldwide network."

Max stared at the other man. "And who is this woman who's my supposed wife?"

"She works for DHS as an Intelligence Operations Specialist. Analyzes chatter coming in. She's the one who first picked up on this. When she did, she was moved onto the Bone Frog staff so we could keep the people in the loop as few as possible. She's been thoroughly briefed ln everything and will be a big help."

Right. Some computer analyst who probably thought this would be a walk in the park.

"I assume she looks enough like the new Mrs. Ferren to pass for her?"

"Even more than we could have hoped for. We were able to scrub whatever is out there on the Internet, but I'm sure this group already has printouts with her picture. They leave nothing to chance. It's a given when your plan is to take over the world."

"What's her name, anyway?"

"Regan Shaw. Another reason she fits the bill. Max Ferren's wife is also named Regan. How bizarre is it that both first names, yours and hers, fit? We figure it's some kind of sign."

"One can pray." He rubbed his jaw. "I just hope she knows enough to make this charade work."

"Don't write her off before you meet her," Si joked. "You might be in for a surprise."

"We'll see," was all Max said.

Chapter Two

A large black Bell 525 chopper with no markings picked them up at exactly one o'clock the next day. After one stop for refueling, the helo landed them on a horse farm at about five thirty in the afternoon. Max spent most of the time on the trip reviewing the material on a tablet Si handed him when he arrived. He was impressed with the amount of wealth and power that would be represented at this gathering and realized how important it was not to forget one little detail that involved these people.

A black SUV with blacked out windows—Max wondered if the government only had one color for every means of transportation—waited to transport them to the house. As they pulled up to a gate set into heavy fieldstone posts, the driver punched a code into the security box, and the massive sections of the gate swung open.

"The entire perimeter of the grounds is connected to the security system, too," Si told him. "That gate we just drove through can be electrified with a punch of a button if someone tries to climb it. Plus, there are ten cameras strategically placed, all monitored both at the house and at the headquarters of the security firm that's on permanent retainer."

Max looked at his friend. "These are no ordinary rich people, Si."

Si shook his head. "No, they're not. In fact, I can't even tell you the reason for all this security. Just suffice it to say, this is the safest place in this area for us to have this meeting."

The vehicle drove directly into the garage and, moments later, Si was showing him to the massive bedroom that would be his for the next five days.

"I opted out of taking you to D.C. itself," Si explained. "Since we don't know who the top dog is yet, the one who we assume expects to rule the world, I didn't want to put you in a position where someone might ask questions."

"Smart." Max nodded and looked around. "Anyway, I'm sure whatever you had doesn't compare to this."

The best description he could come up with for the enormous house was sparsely opulent. From the vast great room that looked out on immaculate landscaping to the kitchen with every conceivable appliance to the en suite bedrooms that surpassed any hotel he'd ever stayed in, the place spelled money and lots of it.

"I hope you guys didn't have to pay rent for this," he joked.

Si grinned. "It belongs to people with old money who don't like interlopers trying to take over their country. All my boss had to do was ask, and it was ours."

Max nodded. "I think I can handle it here."

"Good, because you and your new wife will be here for five days being briefed and getting to know each other."

Max could hardly wait. When he'd been bemoaning the lack of female companionship in his life, this wasn't exactly what he'd meant.

Si and another person from his office spent the afternoon and a good part of the evening giving him background on the cabal whose meeting he'd be attending.

The next morning, he was barely out of the shower, dressed, and in the great room drinking coffee when Si arrived with the same man he'd been with yesterday, carrying a large supply of pastries from something called Morning Glory.

"Do I have to leave some for anyone else?" Max joked, his mouth watering.

"You'd better. This is Regan's favorite bakery, and she might take your head off if you don't."

Great, he thought. A computer nerd whose favorite place was a bakery with a cutesy name and who hoarded pastries. It was a good thing this secret meeting he was going to was only planned for a few days. He'd have to get all the information and get out as fast as possible.

"So, where is my pseudo wife, anyway?" Max picked up a glazed pastry puff with a cream filling and took a bite of it. Holy shit! His taste buds began doing a happy dance. Si hadn't been kidding about the quality of the goods. "She'd better hurry if she wants any of these goodies."

"There'd better be some for me," a female voice called out, "or this project is called off."

Si laughed. "I figured I'd shoot him if he ate too many."

Max looked up as three people came through the front door and into the great room. He thought it was a good thing he had put down his coffee mug, or he'd have spilled the liquid all over himself. He took a deep breath to steady himself. Si had shown him a picture of Regan Shaw on the helo ride from Maine, but a casual phone shot did not do her justice. All he could think now as she walked into the room was, Holy fuck! *This* is my wife?

His mouth went dry, and his breath caught in his throat. He couldn't remember the last time, if ever, a woman had this kind of impact on him. This was no military groupie or a self-involved woman looking for a night of hot sex. He was instantly hard, his cock pressing against the fly of his slacks, a reaction he hadn't had to any female in too long a time. Even his balls tingled. He might have to find a moment to take himself in hand so he didn't attack her the minute they were alone.

He guessed her height to be about five foot six. The dark-green sweater and beige slacks she wore, although not tight or clinging, still did little to disguise her lusciously rounded body, hitting her breasts and hips at just the right angle. Auburn hair fell in soft waves to her shoulders, framing a heart-shaped face with creamy skin. This was no office nerd or timid techno geek. This was a woman, with a capital W.

His mouth watered just at the sight of her. Instead of worrying about how he was going to pass her off as his wife, he was more concerned with being able to keep his hands to himself. He couldn't remember the last time he'd reacted to a woman this way. It was...well...okay, never. He'd had many women that made him hot and horny. But none had ever caused a full body reaction like this one.

Si bent his head to whisper in his ear. "Put your tongue back in your mouth, Max. Better men than you have lusted after her. No deal."

"I'm not—"

But that was as far as he got. The woman came toward him, smiling warmly and holding out her hand.

"Regan Shaw," she told him. "I'm happy to meet you. I understand we're going to be married?"

Max nearly swallowed his tongue while Si just laughed out loud.

"Your wife's not shy," he joked.

"I see that." Max held her hand perhaps a shade longer than he should. It was firm, and there was strength in her grip, but the skin was soft. Enticing.

Jesus, Max. Get a grip, and not on her hand. Or any other part of her body.

He released it and took a step back, just as the front door opened again and two more men entered the house.

"We having a party?" he asked Si under his breath.

"If only. Come on. Let me introduce you to the rest of the crew."

Five minutes later, Max found himself seated at the big dining room table, a mug of coffee at hand and two platters of mouthwatering pastries set out on the table. He couldn't help noticing that Regan Shaw had two of them on a plate in front of her. Interesting. Every woman he'd ever known had avoided food like that as if it was poison. Either she didn't care, or she worked out like crazy. Or was she one of those lucky people with a racing metabolism.

Si leaned over and whispered, "She works out every day. She could probably take you in two out of three falls."

Max raised an eyebrow. But Si had already turned away from him, facing everyone seated there.

"I don't have to tell the rest of you why we're here or what's going on, but before we go any further, let me introduce you to Max DiSalvo, Commander, United States Navy SEALs, Retired. Max." He turned. "Meet the team—Kevin Markham, George Lorenzan and, yes, your newly minted wife, Regan Shaw."

Max nodded. "Happy to meet you."

"The first thing we need to do is bring Max up to speed."

"I thought you did that when you went to Maine," Kevin Markham said.

"I gave him the nuts and bolts, but we need to fill in the spaces." He paused. "First, however, I have a piece of information that Regan picked up just last night. Regan. Let me give Max your credentials and then you have the floor. You're the one who discovered this ugly little plot."

She nodded. "Have at it."

"Okay, Max. Regan has been with Bone Frog for about a year and a half. She was working at Naval Station Norfolk as an analyst until Homeland Security discovered her skills and brought her to Washington. When she tuned into this particular disaster, we stole her for Bone Frog."

Max lifted an eyebrow and looked at the woman. "How long have you been doing this?"

"Altogether?" She wet her lips. "Twenty years."

Max's cock flexed and he had to swallow a moan. "That's a long time."

She nodded. "My husband was based out of there. I had a degree in computer science and a specialty in languages. They were looking for someone who could track chatter, and a friend opened doors for me." She swallowed. "After Dylan was killed, it just made sense for me to keep my job. I had a circle of friends in the area, and I really liked my job. At least I felt as if in some small way I was helping him and his team. Doing something to get the people who killed him. It gave me a tremendous feeling of satisfaction, especially when I found out I had a knack for it."

Her husband was killed? Max wondered how long ago.

"She has a gift for plucking information from out there and making sense of it," Si told him.

"I'm sorry about your husband," he told her.

"Thank you, but the possibility of it was something always in the back of our minds. The nature of his work, you know." She ran her tongue over her lips again.

Max was sure if she did it too often, he'd come just sitting there. Damn. This was what abstinence did to you.

"Would it be inappropriate for me to ask what he did and how he was killed?"

"He was a SEAL," Si told him. "Like you. His team was ambushed on a mission, and everyone was killed. Regan's got incredible skills, and she insisted she could find whatever information the Navy was looking for to see how the disaster happened and why. She knew how to search and what to look for, and went after it with ferocious determination." His smile was anything but humorous. "She was as good as her word. After that, there was no question of her leaving."

Max looked at Regan. "Can I ask how long ago that was?"

"Twenty years. My husband was twenty-four when he was killed."

Max felt as if someone had punched him in the gut. She'd been a widow for twenty years? Devoting her life to helping take down bad guys who were very dangerous? Well, damn!

"I don't know what to say," he told her, "except I know we are all grateful to you."

She shook her head. "I don't want gratitude. I want to get as many of these bastards as I can. My husband died, like many others, to prevent people like this from gaining control of our country. I want to help in any way to make sure they didn't die in vain."

"Okay," Si broke in. "I think we're all in agreement here. What we need to do now, Max, is share with you all the information Regan discovered plus everything we've learned. It won't make you happy, especially this latest bit."

Max leaned forward. "Then we'd better get started."

While George Lorenzan busied himself setting up

electronic equipment, Regan looked around at everyone.

"Last night I plucked some additional bits of conversation out of the stratosphere that frightened even me. We can definitely confirm that it's going to happen on July 4th."

Kevin whistled. "Holy shit! This country will be filled with targets of hundreds of thousands of people celebrating the holiday. I hate to even think of what can happen."

Si nodded. "That means our married couple here has to be thoroughly drilled so they can pass muster, get into the three-day meeting, find out what's going on, and make sure we know about it ASAP." He nodded at Kevin who plucked sheets of paper from a folder and handed them around. "These are the people involved. They have the money to finance this without any outside help. That's one of the reasons this is so easy for them. However, as an added benefit, the Alvaros also are connected to one of the largest drug cartels. There's probably an unlimited supply of funds available from that source."

"Will they be at this little get-together?" Max asked.

Si shook his head. "Luis Rojas isn't part of the core

group. He is keeping a low profile, at least for now. But be aware he could insert himself more visibly at any time. Your job, and Regan's, is to get to this meeting, get pictures of everyone there so we have proof of their participation, record what you can so we have the evidence we need, the location of whatever they have planned, and get the fuck out of there. Once we have that info, we can proceed to set up protection for the target sites, although we really need to stop this before it gets any further. The protection is in case something falls through the cracks. Once we have the information, however, we can move forward to arrest this unholy group."

"You'll need a shitload of proof if they're as wealthy and connected as you tell me," Max pointed out. "They'll have the best attorneys putting up roadblocks."

Si nodded. "Exactly. Okay, Regan, the floor is yours."

Regan Shaw moved to the head of the table, opened a slim laptop, and searched until she found the file she wanted then clicked to open it. A photo popped up on the screen.

"Jed Whitlow, the nominal leader of the group, and his wife Anna."

She took them through each of the people who made up the cabal, explaining who each of them were.

"Being rich isn't enough for them?" Kevin asked, his tone edged with sarcasm.

"It isn't the money," Regan told him. "It's about the power. That's what drives them and what made them bond together."

She clicked again, and a timeline filled the screen that had been set up.

"Si, you already know all of this." She looked at the other two men. "George and Kevin, you know most of this, also. But since you gentlemen are to be the lead in our backup, Si and I agreed you can't hear it too often."

The tall blond who had been introduced as Kevin nodded his head. "We want everything you've got to help you take down these fuckers. I can't wait to get my hands on the traitor who thinks he'd be stepping in to head all this up."

Regan nodded. "I know just how you feel. Si, I think you should go first, laying down the background on this and letting us know what caused us to dig deeper. I'll get the rest of this ready."

Si nodded, took a swallow of coffee, and set his cup down.

"It all started when the DEA got a tip from one of its informants about unusual activity around some of the largest ranches in Texas, Utah, New Mexico, and Arizona."

"What kind of activity?" Max wanted to know.

"The owners were getting more unusual visits from the high-level drug dealers from Mexico. In particular, one dealer, Luis Rojas, the leader of the second-largest cartel. Their interest grew when he began visiting the ranch of Lorena and Elias Alvaro on a regular basis, often bringing his usual group of thugs. What, they wondered, did so-called respectable ranchers want with scum like that? And where did the little group go while he visited with his hosts? And then we learned there was similar activity on huge ranches in nearby states."

Si leaned forward. "We were able to get a couple of men in place as hands on two of the ranches. It took a few months for them to sufficiently snoop around, but eventually they managed to find out that their bosses were providing delivery paths for drugs and getting a fat cut for their troubles. But that was the least of it. It also came to our attention that the owners of all these ranches were meeting on a regular basis. Social? Maybe, but it felt like something else, especially, with the cartel involved."

"Our question," Steve injected, "was what the hell were they discussing? More drugs? Sex trafficking? I mean, shit! These were uber wealthy ranchers who hobnobbed with the cream of society. Their ranches and mineral rights were making them more money than they could spend. What the hell was going on?"

"That's where Regan came in," Si said. "When she picked up on this and the information was passed along to my boss and then to me, I knew she'd be a critical part of our crew. Someone who could pick up chatter and make sense of it. DHS called Norfolk to see if we could borrow her." He grinned. "They don't know we're never giving her back. Okay, Regan, it's yours again."

Flipping through screen after screen, she showed how she'd gathered the bits and pieces and put them together into a whole document. And that, as Si pointed out, scared the crap out of them.

Regan took up the explanation. "I began by analyzing the snippets of chatter coming in about Rojas and about something besides drugs. Then we picked up pieces of conversations coming from overseas that mentioned not only Rojas but also these others. That was just too weird. I analyze words and phrase patterns, and there seemed to be conversations not related to drugs or any other of the usual kinds of traffic. Like this."

She clicked a tiny remote, and phrases appeared on the screen, their meaning chilling Max to the bone.

"I was picking up a tiny smattering here and there that made my skin prickle," she continued. "Pieces about high-value terrorists and how the Rojas cartel was helping to smuggle them. Certain phrases. Words I knew they used as codes. The ranches involved were being used as way stations for these terrorists. Rojas would deliver them to one of the ranches, and they'd be processed from there. At the same time, we noticed the ranch owners gathering for regular meetings once a month. The more I put it together, the more it frightened me."

"When we laid it all out," Si interjected, "we had a picture that scared the shit out of all of us at Homeland Security." He looked at Regan. "Bring up the diagram."

She clicked through to the next screen. "Take a look. What we have is a situation where the terrorist leaders are brought into Mexico and smuggled into this country by the cartel. Each of them in his own right is a highly trained, highly motivated terrorist leader responsible for some of the most horrendous actions in the Middle East."

She clicked again, and a map of the United States came up.

"DHS has developed a key-areas map, marking places that terrorist groups could attack where their actions would do the worst damage. It would also leave a leadership vacuum, and they would be able to take over. We were pretty damn sure they would only be able to control certain areas, although that was bad enough." She looked around the table, her eyes coming to rest on Max. "Then we put together the meetings these ranchers held on a regular basis with the influx of these barbarians and the increased chatter we picked up and realized they were plotting to use these thugs for their own purposes. There would be a network spread across the country, directed by a group of very rich, very powerful people who would use the terrorists to control the population. They'd be able to take over and be in complete control. An unholy cabal."

"We think their ultimate goal is global control," Si added. "That's the opinion of the experts, and I actually agree with them."

Max felt a chill race down his spine. "You're referring to the group I'm going to be meeting with?"

Regan was the one who answered. "They each have untold wealth and global influence and are avidly power hungry."

"Jesus Christ." The words were said softly but no less effectively.

Si nodded. "Exactly. You have five days to memorize everything we have on these people as well as everything about Max Ferren's life before jumping into this. As I told both of you, you guys resemble the real couple so strongly it's uncanny. That's what gave us the idea to do this. No one will be questioning you, especially once you get those background folders down pat."

"We can do it." Max knew all about playing a part to accomplish a mission.

Silas gave Max a penetrating stare. "Your job is to get the evidence to put these people away. That's why we wanted someone with SEAL experience. SEALs have had the most interaction with terrorists and know how they think and act. But it couldn't be someone on active duty."

Max sat there, gripped by the familiar feeling of preparing for a mission, except he knew in his soul this trumped any other mission he'd ever taken part in.

"Also," Si added, "you and Regan need to take this

short time to really get to know each other as a married couple would. There can't be any reason to make these people suspicious."

Max glanced over at Regan, whose full lips were curved in a tiny smile. "Don't worry, Max. That'll be the fun part of this operation."

That's what he was afraid of.

Chapter Three

Regan was the central point of information as they spent the morning going over the basic facts as they knew them so everyone had as comprehensive a picture of the situation as possible. Everyone had questions about the people involved and how the extraction would work if it had to happen before the three-day meeting was over. She and Si answered all of them.

George and Kevin would be the backup crew, monitoring any calls from the special phones Max and Regan would have if they couldn't get through to Si, and constantly in touch with any resources they might need. They were also working with an unexpected bonus on the ground. In checking all key personnel in the area, he'd discovered that Lou Valenti, the county sheriff, was also a former SEAL. He'd gotten clearance to be read in, and the man had nearly been shocked out of his shorts.

"Jed Whitlow and his wife have owned that hunting lodge forever," he'd told Si. "They're around a lot during hunting season, but in the past couple of years they've entertained guests for a few days every few months. Was this what they were planning the whole time they've been here?"

"Appears so," he confirmed. "It's a long story how this particular group got together and I'll fill you in on that. But for now, you need to keep this between us and assure me you're here if we need you."

"That's not a problem. But if we're going to meet again, I'd just as soon we did it in the next county. These people are obsessive about their privacy, and now I can see why. We don't want them to know you and I are connected in any way."

"So that's what we did," Si told everyone after filling them in. "We actually met up two counties away in a strip club, believe it or not. Lou knows the owner, and he let us use his office. Lou will be our boots on the ground in the target location."

This afternoon, they'd begin to drill Max and Regan on each of the couples involved in this heinous cabal. It was important the two of them be aware of everything the real Max Ferren would know. These people didn't like surprises, and they'd be on the alert for anything the least off-kilter.

When they broke for lunch, Si doled out the room assignments, except for Max who already had his.

Regan grabbed her suitcase from the front hall and was about to head up the stairs when a warm, rough, masculine hand closed over hers.

"I've got it." The voice had the same rough edge to it.

Strong fingers gripped the handle of her suitcase, and the faint scent of aftershave with a hint of the outdoors in it tickled her nose.

"I— Oh! Okay. Thanks."

A muscular arm pressed against hers, the warmth of it penetrating her skin. Max DiSalvo was so close she could count the whiskers in his three-day stubble beard, a style that accented his rugged jaw and lean face and matched his close-cropped salt-and-pepper hair. A faint tingle raced through her, almost unfamiliar it had been so long since she'd felt it.

She slid a sideways glance at him as they climbed the stairs to the second floor. She guessed his height at six feet, and his lean, muscular body spoke of his years as a SEAL and the physical work he did since his retirement from the service. Si had certainly picked a good-looking husband for her. She just had to remember that this was all strictly business, and serious business at that. And that he'd been chosen as much for his particular skills as for his uncanny resemblance to Max Ferren. She wondered which of them he'd be called upon to use.

She thought about the days ahead of them. This was her first live mission, so to speak. A lot of years had passed since her husband was killed on a special mission and she'd chosen to fight on in his memory, using the skills she had. When she'd detected the first threads of this heinous plot, she'd been sick to her stomach. The more she discovered, the worse it got. An elite group of obnoxiously wealthy people looking to take over the United States and run it like many Middle Eastern countries under the thumb of the worst terrorists they smuggled into this country.

When Si had asked her to take an active role, she'd been unsure at first if she could carry it off. It wasn't, after all, what she usually did. But then the idea of personally helping to take these people down washed away any reservations she had. Now her only worry was how she was going to carry off the role of Max's wife. She had seen his photo, of course, when Si showed her pictures of both men. The similarities were uncanny. What she hadn't been prepared for, however, was the sexual magnetism of Max DiSalvo in person. Walking beside him now, she mentally fanned her face.

Get it together, Regan. This is a job and a damned important one. You're not a hormone-heavy girl anymore.

Unfortunately her hormones that had been in the deep freeze had decided to wake up on their own and start doing a dance, and at the most inappropriate time. This wasn't who she was at all. She was here on serious business, thrilled to be chosen for this role, so she'd better get her act together. Their deadline was closer than they'd expected.

"I got my room assignment yesterday when I arrived," Max told her, waving her toward a large bedroom. "Si said he was putting us next door to each other." He chuckled. "So we could start getting to know each other. A teasing little joke on his part."

Regan looked around. "Wow!"

The bedroom was bigger than the living room in her apartment, and the bed was big enough for a slumber party. Everything was done in soft shades of blue and gold that eased her nervous edge at once. A partially open door led to an en suite bath.

He grinned. "Si wasn't kidding when he said the people who owned this had a bunch of money."

"I know," she agreed. "We could probably hold a dance in the living room. I don't usually come into contact with people in this environment."

Max quirked an eyebrow at her. "You don't go to D.C. parties? Or handle missions like this at all?"

She shook her head and gave a short laugh. "No, I'm not on the A-list for D.C. social activities. And my work has basically been confined to computers and other electronic equipment and analyzing the results of what I find. I spend a lot of time hanging out with computer nerds and translators, deciphering stuff."

"And you like that?" He shook his head. "Stupid question. You must, or you wouldn't do it."

"The answer is yes. It probably sounds boring to an action man like you, but I love taking all the different bits and pieces of things and making them part of a whole. I helped find the information for the mission that took down those bastards who murdered Dylan." Her smile had little humor in it. "After that, it was a way to get past his death. Then it just became a way of life. Every tiny bit of information I discovered was a small victory for me."

Max nodded. "Dylan was a lucky man."

"I was the lucky one." She shrugged. "But you aren't here to discuss me."

Max shook his head. "On the contrary. With a possible target date of July 4th, every minute and every bit of information that frames our mission is critical. If we're going to be husband and wife, the more we know about each other, the easier it will be to pull it off. In fact, I believe Si has time blocked out after everything else for us to learn everything we can about each other."

"Everything?" Okay, she sounded like an idiot.

Max studied her face for a long moment, something mysterious in his eyes. Then he grinned. "Everything we care to share. How's that? Meanwhile, I'm in the next room. Let me get myself out of here so you can unpack and we can get down to lunch."

Regan watched him walk from the room and couldn't keep from admiring his lean muscular build. The way the slacks fit his long legs and his tight butt. There was something so powerful, so magnetic about him, and she wondered if he knew he exuded sex appeal. Si had not told her anything about his personal life except he was single and ran a commercial fishing company. Why wasn't he married? Had he ever been? Had his wife been one of those who loved the status of being married to a man in the military but hated dealing with the realities? Regan had sure seen plenty of them.

It took a long time after Dylan's death before she

even dipped her toe into the dating waters. Mostly her experiences had been...nice. A bland word that perfectly described the situation. But there was something about Max DiSalvo that made her hormones do a little tap dance. Would the temptation he presented be too great for her? Or maybe she was the only one having inappropriate thoughts. They were here to carry out an urgent mission. She was sure he had nothing else but that on his mind.

Get your brain together, Regan. You're here on a matter of national security.

That was primary. She had twenty-plus years of discipline to call on, and she wasn't about to let Si down because she'd suddenly turned into a horny teenager. Still...

Swallowing a sigh, she went about the business of unpacking her clothes and taking a few moments to freshen up in the bathroom. It was going to be a long afternoon.

*****

Max let out a long breath. What the hell was wrong with him? Even when he was deliberately looking for female companionship, he didn't have this kind of reaction to someone. Sometimes he wished he did, and that his dick was a little more enthusiastic about some of the women he chose to spend his free time with.

Not that that particular organ had shirked his duty when it was clothes off and onto the mattress. But he'd made up his mind he couldn't give the proper attention to a relationship while he was still in the SEALs. And, in retirement, he'd finally realized that just having sex as an exercise didn't have the excitement it once did. As the rest of his life stretched out before him, he finally understood that he wanted what many of his friends had. What Si had. A woman he connected with on all levels who wanted to share his life with him. But why did she have to be the one he was going into a dangerous mission with?

They'd have to make sure they convinced the people in the cabal they were in fact a real married couple. Could they do that and leave sex out of the picture?

Jackass. You don't even know if she's attracted to you, and this is for sure not the time to find out. Stick to business.

He washed up in the bathroom then opened the special suitcase he'd brought. Si had told him to bring everything he'd need for this meeting plus the one with the cabal. He certainly had whatever would be required, although he hoped he wouldn't have to use them. He glanced over the toys he'd packed—a Glock 17 with several boxes of ammo plus a Browning SA-22 grade one takedown rifle, so-called because it can be taken apart and carried in a small canvas bag. He'd also packed his Ka-Bar utility knife, in case he got into some close quarters situations.

A knock sounded on the door and, when he looked up, he saw Si in the doorway, a hard-sided suitcase in one hand, looking at him with a raised eyebrow.

"If you're asking to come in, the door's open, right?"

Si wandered over to the open suitcase and studied the weapons Max had placed on the bed. "I see you brought your toys with you."

"Never leave home without them."

"I have some additional goodies for you," Si told him. "Some Ferren Industries weapons." "They'll think it's strange if you don't bring any of those with you, so I have a few here for you to show them."

"Because I need those with the Ferren name on them?"

"Yes. Believe it or not, there's a target range at the back end of this property."

Max barked a laugh. "Nothing about this place

would surprise me at this point."

"We'll block out some time to get you and Regan some target practice so you both can get a feel for them."

"The wives shoot, too?"

Si chuckled. "Oh, yeah. Wait until you meet them. Oh, and Regan knows her way around guns. No worries there."

"Good to know. I always wanted a wife who could shoot straight." Then he frowned. "Are you saying they'll expect me to demonstrate the efficiency of these weapons?"

Si nodded. "Most likely. Remember. They're going to arm these fucking terrorists they've been smuggling into this country. Regan has pieced together enough chatter to know they're planning simultaneous attacks in well-populated areas. Ferren was also getting them explosives, but we'll take care of that. I don't know if they have any of the guns at the lodge, just to see what's being used. If they do, just in case, only the ones you demonstrate will work. The firing pins will have been removed. But that should be no problem for you. There hasn't been a weapon made yet that you couldn't handle in less than five minutes."

Max shook his head. "Jesus Christ, Si. Who the

fuck are these people?"

"We'll be starting to review them after lunch. You won't believe half this shit."

"But I'll bet I will."

They both turned to see Regan standing in the doorway.

"That's right," Si agreed. "You did the initial workup when you first pieced this together."

She shook her head. "It still makes me sick that people who have untold wealth and power because of this country want to destroy it."

"How did they all get together?" Max asked. "Si, that's one thing you never explained when you gave me the rundown."

"I wanted to wait until I could lay it all out for both of you at the same time." He glanced at his watch. "Come on. I think lunch is ready. Let's eat and get back to business."

The lunch was delicious, but Max noticed he wasn't the only one eager to finish and get on with things. Once the dishes were cleared away, Silas turned the laptop on again, and once more set up the small screen at the end of the table.

"Let's begin with the Whitlows, Jed and Anna. Their place is in Utah near the Four Corners, as it's called, where Arizona, Colorado, Utah, and New Mexico touch."

He hit a key, and a picture of the couple popped up on the screen. Jed had close-cropped, curly gray hair and a long face, dominated by a hawk-like nose. Anna, on the other hand, seemed shorter than he was, almost petite, with blonde hair that fell to her rounded jawline. Her face was set in a look of arrogance. Max disliked her at once and wondered if she was like this in person.

Si went on to describe the size of their wealth and the connections they had. "It still surprises me that no matter how much money some people have, it's never enough. In the past five years, they've made millions from the Rojas cartel smuggling both people and goods into this country, using Whitlow's land as a distribution point."

This kind of business always made Max sick to his stomach. The human misery that resulted from it just kept rising, but the people making money just kept on keeping on. Why shut off the money stream, right?

Si clicked through the rest of the group. Gavin and Elizabeth Emery were both in their early fifties. Their ranch was in New Mexico.

Another click and they were looking at Lorena

Alvaro and her husband, Elias.

"She's the link to the cartel," Si told them. "Well, actually her husband is. Their ranch is two hundred and fifty thousand acres, located in the southwest corner of Arizona so it bumps up against both California and the Mexican state of Sonora."

"Very convenient," Max commented.

"Sure is. For decades they've been collecting a king's ransom from the cartels for allowing them to use their land as a direct route to smuggle drugs and even people into the country. Apparently the arrangement began with his grandfather who came here with millions from the drug business and bought this ranch. When ownership changed, the situation barely missed a beat. Except I understand the ante was upped. Lorena is a greedy bitch."

"Greedy is right." Regan shook her head. "You'd think the millions they've made in ranching and investments would be enough for her."

"For some people," Si pointed out, "there's no such thing as enough."

"Question." Max looked down at the open folder in front of him. "According to this info you gave us, she's really the one who calls the shots in this nasty little group."

Si nodded. "Jed Whitlow thinks he's in charge but he's fooling himself. That woman is tougher and more heartless than most of the men I've met in my life. She's hungry for power, and I'm not even sure if taking over this country will satisfy her."

"Jesus." Max blew out a breath. "Those are the worst kind of people. Heartless, soulless, and feeding on power and control. Other people's lives mean nothing to them."

"You got that right. In many ways like the tribal leaders you knocked heads with in the sandbox. Human life, except their own, means nothing to them. Money and power. Those are their drugs."

"And they don't care who they kill to get it," Kevin added. "I've seen more situations like this than I can count. Too many of them."

"Next up are the Cavanaughs, Kurt and Hildie. Their ranch is in Colorado and has been in the family for four generations. Besides thriving in the beef industry, they have mineral-rich land which has provided a steady stream of royalties for the rights.

"And finally, we have the Ferrens." He looked at Max and Regan. "Bernardo is the only anomaly. He's not a rancher. As we dug into the history of each of them, we learned he and Jed Whitlow are friends from college who have kept in touch all these years. He and his brother own Ferren Arms Manufacturing in Colorado. They produce handguns similar to the Glock and four different models of rifles, including a sniper rifle that's supposed to be the best thing on the market. Jed reached out to him when this little group got past the stage of kicking ideas around."

George raked his fingers through his hair. "Jesus Christ!"

"Exactly."

"How did they all connect?" Max wanted to know. "The original four, I mean."

"I can answer that," Regan told hm. "I started researching them as soon as the first bits of chatter came across my desk. It seems they were all at a regional cattlemen's convention. They didn't usually attend them anymore, but this particular one was for people in the same financial category as theirs. The meeting was to discuss restrictive government regulations as they applied to ranching, especially water rights. Somehow, probably from comments they'd all made in the meetings, the four couples gravitated toward each other, and that's when the genesis of the plan from hell was formed."

"Lorena also saw another way to use the power of

the cartel her husband had a connection with." Si clicked to bring up another screen.

Several ugly faces stared out at them. To Max, they looked like the high-value targets he and his team had been tasked with either capturing or killing. A chill slithered down his spine, knowing firsthand how vicious they were. Soulless, despite their proclamations to the contrary.

"He used them," Si continued, "to smuggle the terrorists into this country."

"If their plan is to stage simultaneous bloodbaths around the country," Max asked, "what comes after that?"

"Disruption of law enforcement and the military," Si told him. "Putting their own people in place. Creating their own version of a military state where they control all the money and resources."

"It has to have taken a long time for them to put this together," George spoke up for the first time.

Si nodded. "That convention was five years ago. We believe they have been meeting regularly ever since. Developing resources. Funding places for the devils they're smuggling into this country to prepare and wait."

"You told me they have someone in place to step

into the leadership role," Max reminded him, "but you haven't identified him yet."

Si nodded. "My bosses at DHS have three possible, but we can't pin down which one of them it is. All of them are unhappy with the current administration. They believe they've been shunted aside. Given weak roles in the administration. Had their power diluted. When you have a president as confident and take-charge as this one, he's going to make enemies. In both parties, I might add."

Max refilled his coffee mug from the carafe on the table. "So, let me get this straight. A bunch of people with too much money and egos bigger than the Atlantic Ocean get their noses out of joint at the way the government regulates their industry. They decide they'll take over the country and run it for their benefit. Have I got that right?"

"Except for one thing." Si looked from one to other of the people at the table. "Some of what we picked up Regan has interpreted in a way that makes my stomach climb my backbone. Once they've got the good old U. S. of A., they plan to expand to other countries including Mexico, and put it in the hands of the cartels, at least more than it is now. And maybe the Middle East, so the soulless terrorists they're importing for their big blowup here can have their revenge on the countries shutting them down."

The silence around the table was so thick Max was sure he could cut it with a knife.

"Holy mother fucking god." He almost whispered the words. "And this meeting Regan and I are attending is, what, the final gathering before the first big event?"

Si nodded.

"Well, then, we'd best get on with this session. I want every detail, and I mean every single one, that you've got on all the people involved. I want to know how our backup will work, how we contact you, what our extraction is if we need it. You and me, Si. We'll plan this like a regular SEAL mission. It's the only way it has a chance to succeed."

Chapter Four

Max stood on the back patio, staring out at the vast expanse of green lawn that stretched away from the house. Trees stood as tall sentinels bordering each side, and he knew that beyond them was electrified fencing with concertina wire on the top. He knew it because Si had given him the video tour of the property and pointed out all the security measures. For a moment, he wished he could drag all these people he and Regan would be meeting with back to this house and beat the shit out of them until they were bloody and broken. What kind of people were they who would turn on their own country that way?

He heard the sliding door open behind him and turned to see Regan step out onto the patio. Despite the intensity of the day-long session, and the stomach-turning events and people they were discussing, she still looked cool and contained. The only indication of its effect on her were the faint lines of strain at the corners of her eyes and her mouth. She carried a tablet in her hand similar to the one Si had given Max the day before.

"Mind if I join you?" she asked.

"Absolutely not." He smiled. "In fact, I should be getting acquainted with my wife."

She chuckled. "I'm curious as to how this will all work. I've never done this before."

He cocked an eyebrow. "Played a role? Pretended to be someone you aren't?"

She shook her head. "Like I said earlier today, I'm the most comfortable working inside."

"Well, you've done a hell of a job ferreting this out." He lifted his glass in a toast. "Without you, this plot never would have come to light, and this country would be hit with a massive disaster. Caught totally unaware."

"If what Si learned is true and they have whatever this is set for the Fourth of July, we can't afford to make one mistake at this meeting."

He nodded. "No kidding. The Fourth of July—Independence Day—is coming up in three weeks. That means they'll be planning the final details in this meeting. I don't know what kind of security they have at this place we're going to, but I'll need to find a way to slip off in the evening and reach out to Si."

"It'll be tricky," she pointed out, "but we'll figure it out. The first thing we'll need to do is check the security they have in place. See if it's all electronic or if they have flesh-and-blood security men hanging around."

"Remember, we have one more test to pass before we even get to that," he reminded her. "We have to check into the hotel in the town near this lodge and meet with Whitlow. Apparently he's promised to give them a full assessment of us to make sure we won't cause a problem before he lets us into the inner circle."

"But Bernardo vouched for us. Si made sure of that when he saw him." She frowned.

"However, I'll bet everyone in this little group is nervous since Bernardo's 'heart attack' happened."

Max snorted. "I'm surprised he didn't have a real one when Si walked into his office and told him we had the goods on him for his illegal arms sales. And that we'd frozen all his offshore accounts."

"And *I'm* surprised he didn't just pick up the phone and call for his attorney," she told him.

Max actually chuckled. "I think when someone comes to your home at six in the morning with a Homeland Security Badge, two FBI agents, and a folder full of paperwork including your offshore bank accounts, you have a good idea a lawyer isn't going to help. Si told me it was a tossup who he was more afraid of, Si and his merry band or the people in this little group. You can bet that, weapons or not, these so-called friends would have disposed of him where no one would find him. They don't want this kind of thing spilling over onto them."

"Si said Bernardo did a masterful job of convincing Jed Whitlow his heart attack was real and that his brother could be trusted."

Max frowned. "I hope his wife isn't a loose cannon."

Regan shook her head. "As I understand it, she's so afraid her high-society friends will find out her husband is on the verge of going to prison, she was willing to do anything."

"They aren't really going to let him off, are they?" Max asked.

"Not completely. But it's up to DHS what happens to him when we get this wrapped up."

Max drained his glass and glanced at Regan. "Can I get you something? I'm drinking plain soda but perhaps wine? Or whatever?"

"Soda for me, too. Thanks. And we probably should get to work on that thick folder Si handed us and learn our parts." She grinned. "Think I'll get an award if I play it right?"

He moved so he was standing close enough that he was looking directly into her eyes. "You'll get more than that if we pull it off. And I personally will buy you anything you like."

She stared back at him, her emerald eyes darkening almost to a forest green before she took a step back. "Well, then. I'll have to start making a list."

In the kitchen, he refilled both their glasses and carried them back out to the patio. Regan was standing there, hands in the pockets of her slacks, just staring off across the lawn much as he'd been doing before. He took a moment to study her, framed by the fading rays of the sun as she was. There was something about her he'd never seen in all the other women who had passed through his life. And that was exactly what they'd done—passed through. His choice, for sure. He hadn't wanted depth, he'd wanted casual sex with no demands. The SEALs got all the rest from him.

But now this woman had come into his life at the exact moment when he didn't need a distraction. He gave thanks she appeared to be a thorough professional who was as focused on this as he was. Still, with the days of playacting facing them, you never knew what could happen. He had to keep remembering all the lives in danger if he screwed up.

He nudged her arm and handed her the filled glass.

"How about we sit down at that table over there and get to know each other a little better outside of the mission parameters."

She looked at him, her lips turned up in a hint of a smile.

"Why, Max, what an interesting proposition."

He shook his head. "That wasn't exactly what I had in mind. Although when this is over, if we survive it, we might address that very situation."

Something heated swirled in her emerald-green eyes, just for a moment, but it woke up feelings in him he didn't know he had. How was it that now, in the midst of this crisis, he had finally met a woman that he might want to share his life with, and he had to tuck it all away? Because he was a SEAL—there was no "former" about it—and that was what SEALs did. But, Jesus. It was going to take every bit of discipline he had to keep his hands to himself. Would one kiss be so bad?

"We should get through this first," she reminded him, interrupting his train of thought.

Good thing, too.

"That's at the top of the list." He sat down in one of the

chairs and motioned her to another one. "And part of that is getting to know each other well enough to pull off our role as a married couple. Make ourselves believable. These people won't be happy with the change, and we'll be under a microscope. If they suspect the least little thing, we'll be dead, and so will a lot of other people."

"You're right." She took a sip of her drink and set the glass down. "Okay, Commander, fire away."

"I'm curious. How did you get into the data mining business to begin with? It isn't, at least in my limited knowledge, a career that's hot in the marketplace."

"I got lucky." She shrugged. "I've always been interested in puzzles of all different kinds. I read some books about people who could listen to fractured conversations, pick out key words, and discern the purpose of the dialogue. I had a double major in college, languages and computer science. And I was fascinated with the military. Always had been. A friend of a friend knew of an opening for someone with my skills. I got an interview, and that was that."

"Where do you get the information you analyze?" He chuckled. "That is, if it's not a national secret."

"If Silas picked you for this mission, I think there's

very little that would be secret from you."

"Thanks for that."

She shifted in her chair, and, when she re-crossed her legs, Max couldn't help noticing the flex of thigh muscles beneath the smooth fabric of her slacks. At another time he'd like to have those thighs clamped around his body, holding him in place. But this was neither the time nor the place, and he had enough discipline to put it all in a corner of his mind. At least for now.

"Some of our information comes from intercepting phone calls—and that I *really* can't tell you about. But, right now, the bulk of it has been coming through what our satellites have picked up and transmitted to us."

"You have to be damn good at what you do if you can take bits and pieces and make this kind of picture out of them."

She grinned at him, and he noticed the faint hint of a dimple he'd missed at the left corner of her mouth.

"I am. But I have a lot of help, too, in deciphering what I come up with. It's really a team effort."

"Teamwork is always the best," he agreed. "Did you get your job at Norfolk after you were married?"

She shook her head. "I was already working there.

I met him through friends one night when we were all at the same bar. He asked me out to dinner, and we never looked back."

"I'm so sorry for your loss." He'd had to say that too many times to widows of SEAL friends, but he still never felt comfortable with it.

"Thank you. We were only married for four years when he was killed, but I was lucky to have him for the time I did."

"There hasn't been anyone since then? Just checking to see if there's someone waiting for you to come back from this mission," he added. "And you know, maybe worrying about you. And that could distract you."

Anger flashed across her face but so quickly he wondered if he'd actually seen it.

"I'm not going to get upset at the question," she said carefully, "because I understand why you have to ask it. However, I would have thought Silas would have told you, prepping you for this mission."

Max watched her carefully. "He did say there wasn't anyone specific in your life, but I always like to check things myself."

She crossed her legs, lifted her glass, and drained it. Then she turned to him.

"I hope you're not playing games, Commander DiSalvo, but I have nothing to hide. I've had one or two short-lived relationships since Dylan was killed and occasional dates here and there, but that's it." Her look was almost defiant. "It's hard finding someone to live up to him. And I'm told I'm very picky."

She sat so stiffly in her chair that Max swallowed a grin. He'd been testing her, but he didn't want to piss her off. She was ideal for this. In addition to her skills and the fact that she was a knockout with a brain, Si had told him she had an excellent memory and retained critical facts.

"So, have I passed the test?" There was a definite edge to her voice.

Max grinned. "More than. Sorry for that. I'm just used to working with the same team all the time, people I'm comfortable with and trust without question. No matter how much Si vouched for you, I had to satisfy myself. You're bright, you're sharp, and you don't rattle. I just had to make sure I wasn't missing anything." He lost the grin. "I've been depending on the same group of men for so many years, I have to learn how to trust others all over again."

The look on her face softened. "I should have

remembered that. Si told me you were a SEAL for almost twenty years."

He nodded. "Twenty being the operative word. I actually had another eighteen months to go."

She wet her lower lip, and he tried not to be fascinated by the quick swipe of her tongue. "He explained about your injury. I'm sorry."

"You don't have to worry about me holding my own. It might not have healed well enough to keep me in the SEALs, but I don't miss a beat anywhere else." He tried to keep the bitterness from his voice.

"I believe that. My turn. Anyone waiting at home for you? Or anywhere else?"

He shook his head and took another swallow of his soft drink. "The truth? I never wanted to start a relationship with anyone all that time. Everything I had belonged to the SEALs. I figured when the time came, I'd have found someone and settled into a pattern that I could just step into after retirement."

She burst out laughing. "Spoken like a true male."

He managed a grin of his own. "I guess. Anyway, I was out of the SEALs before I expected and, well, there it is. My friends worry I'll turn into a grouchy old man."

She tilted her head and studied him. "Somehow, I

don't see that happening. I'm willing to bet there are plenty of women, maybe even a long line of them, who are ready to make sure Max DiSalvo doesn't spend his later years all alone."

"I think you're imagining things. Anyway, that's a discussion for another day. Suffice it to say, no marriages. Not even a fiancée." After this mission was complete and he could explore those reactions his body kept having to her. He hoped things would change.

"So. Now that we've gotten past the *You show me yours and I'll show you mine* dance, we should probably get to the things that will really matter. The things that make us who we are. Things a married couple would know about each other."

"You're right, even though Max Ferren and his wife have only been married for a short time. Second marriage for both of them, and long enough to know each other's quirks and habits. Let me get the folder Si put together that gives us all that information so we can share it. And add some of our own peculiarities so we don't get caught off guard."

They sat there in the waning sun, throwing information back and forth about the people they were about to become, concentrating with the same intensity Regan applied to her complicated job and Max had applied as a SEAL. He thought of other people who so often used the expression life-or-death to describe situations and wondered how many of them even knew what it meant. Three days from now the two of them would face the first of their hurdles when they met Jed Whitlow at the hotel where he'd insisted they stay before heading to the meeting at the lodge. That literally would be life or death. One false step, and he and Regan would both be dead, not to mention untold numbers of people who would be victims of whatever horrific event was being planned.

The sun had set and day was fading to night when Si joined them on the patio carrying his ever-present mug of coffee.

"You kids playing nice with each other?" He smiled while asking.

"Yes, Dad." Max winked at him. "We're sharing our toys and everything."

"We've been doing our getting-to-know-each-other thing," Regan assured him.

Si dropped into a chair at the table where they sat. "Glad to hear it. You'll be walking into a group of people who aren't even sure they trust you being there and who probably are suffering paranoia off the charts because of Bernardo's 'heart attack.'"

"Tomorrow, one of the things we need to prepare is the electronics," Regan reminded him.

A slow grin spread over Si's face. "Anxious to get your hands on those gadgets," he teased.

"You bet." She looked at Max. "I don't know if Silas has told you, but he's got special pens for us, one of which records voice and the other video. They are sound-and-motion activated."

Max knew his eyes lit up. He, too, was big on gadgets. More than once his team had been saved by one. Then he sobered.

"They can't be detectable," he reminded his friend. "I assume we'll be using them at the table or whatever while we're meeting, and you can bet your sweet ass they'll have all kinds of detectors in the room."

Si nodded. "No problem. The material each of them is constructed of blocks any electronic detection. And yes, they've been thoroughly tested. I made sure everyone involved in this project understands the critical nature of it and that there is no room for error."

"Good. I knew you would, but I always check things five times. What about cell phones? I don't imagine the reception is very good there. Plus, if these weasels decide to check them, they'll expect to be looking at the ones used by Max and Regan Ferren, not us."

"We have them for you. They can be packed in the hard-sided compartment in your suitcase with your weapons."

"And where will the real couple be while this is going on?"

"In the same location as Jeanne Ferren, Bernardo's wife, far away from civilization with a full complement of round-the-clock guards. This should all be over before anyone gets suspicious."

"Yeah, let us pray," Regan said.

"Exactly what we are all doing," Si assured her, "while we're taking care of business."

"How about reviewing these profiles with us?" Max asked. He picked up the tablet he'd carried out to the patio with him and left on the table earlier.

"That's just what I was about to suggest. And let me mention this before we get started. It would be great for Regan to take the lead here. Most of the primary members are male, although their spouses are included and active. But Lorena Alvaro is a force of nature, and it would help all around if she had a woman at the table she couldn't pressure or treat with disdain."

“She sounds lovely,” Regan commented, wrinkling her nose.

“I promise you’re more than a match for her.” He looked at Max. “That okay with you?”

Max chuckled. “Whatever works. I for one think if we handle ourselves right with Jed Whitlow, it would throw some interesting dynamics into the situation. They’re probably expecting pale copies of Bernardo Ferren and his wife. If we give them just the opposite, they might end up making mistakes.”

“Good point.” Si stopped and looked from one to the other. “I know I don’t need to say this but make no mistake about this. Getting accepted into this upcoming meeting and finding a way to stop this abomination is the most important thing you will ever do. Otherwise, a great many people will die, and the fabric of this country could be ripped apart. I don’t care how you play it. I chose the two of you not just because you resemble Max Ferren and his wife but because you both have the brains and the experience to pull this off. How you play it is up to you.”

“We’ve got it, Si,” Max assured him, noting that Regan nodded her understanding. “You and I were SEALs for a long time. It’s a fact that SEALs have been involved in every kind of conflict since the beginning.

We took down Osama Bin Laden, the most wanted man in the world. Rescued Captain Phillips. Did a lot of things that will never be written about. We can handle this."

"I hear ya, buddy. Just remember these are terrorists. Not just the people they are bringing into this country but the ones sitting around the table. Terrorism is a tactic, a strategy used to achieve a specific end. In this case it's the weakening of America, by killing people and by creating disarray within the government so they can sweep in and take over. We can't let that happen."

"We're smart, experienced people, Si," Regan told him. "We know what's at stake, and we'll get you what you need to stop it."

He blew out a breath. "Okay. I have faith in you two. Now. Anyone want some coffee before we get started? No? Okay, let me get a refill, and we'll get at it."

Chapter Five

“Yes, Lorena, I’m just walking into the hotel now.”

Jed Whitlow squeezed his cell phone so hard he wondered if it might break. The woman was driving him crazy. Too many times in the past month he’d wondered if it had been a mistake to include the Alvaros in their little group. But Elias Alvaro had been the connection to the cartels, and, without him, smuggling the high-profile terrorists they were using might have been impossible. The woman was just a control freak who was getting on everyone’s nerves. That could not happen. What they had planned was only step one in their blueprint for global domination.

“So you have not met with them yet?” she asked? “Vetted them?”

“Did you just say vetted them? Lorena, this is Bernardo’s brother and his wife. For all intents and purposes, they are already vetted.”

Jed gritted his teeth. The woman had begun to get on his last nerve. With everything at stake and the target date so close, he had to get past that.

“Yes, that is exactly what I said. We cannot take

any chances."

"I told you I just arrived. Their plane only landed two hours ago. They had to get their luggage and pick up their rental car. They texted me when they were on their way. I didn't want to be waiting at their suite with a list of questions in hand. This is not high school."

"You're right, it's not," she snapped. "The future of this country, maybe even the world, depends on how we move forward. We can't afford to include anyone at the last minute who might screw this up. You did speak with them on the phone, right?"

"With Max Ferren? Bernardo's brother? Yes, I did. And I worked the questions we agreed on into the conversation."

"So, tell me how he sounded?"

He wanted to tell her he'd give her a report when he had something to relate, but he knew she, like the others, was on edge because of this last-minute switch. Although he'd given them a full rundown on Max Ferren, he hadn't seen the man in several years. When he and Bernardo got together, it was usually just the two of them. Sometimes their wives joined them, but that was it. Which reminded him that he'd better bring his own wife up to date.

This interview would be the key to deciding if

everything was a go or if—unfortunately—they had to make adjustments, which would be disastrous.

"He sounded like a man trying to control his irritation at the obvious grilling." He snapped out the words. "What would you expect?"

"And the person you have monitoring the suite?" Lorena persisted. "Did anything show up there?"

"No." He snapped the word. "Either they know the suite is bugged, or they're actually who they say they are. Lorena, these are not stupid people. If they are the real deal, as we believe, they could get pissed off and pull out. Where are we going to get a supplier of the quantity of arms on order plus the other items we need on such short notice?"

"I'm just being—"

"Cautious, I know." He pulled in a deep breath and let it out slowly. "Listen. I'm in the hotel now on my way to the elevator. I'm going to hang up, and I'll call you as soon as this meeting is over. Meantime, go have a drink and settle your nerves."

Without waiting for an answer, he disconnected the call. Speaking of nerves, she was certainly getting on his. He was well aware of the fact she was their connection to the cartel. Without them, this operation would be far more difficult. Maybe even impossible.

But sweet Jesus, the woman was a royal pain in the ass. Somehow, he and the others would have to figure out how to forge a connection with the cartel that cut the Alvaros out altogether.

As he strode through the lobby toward the elevator, he scrolled through files until he found the one he was looking at. Max and Regan Ferren had been photographed recently at a high society event in Houston, Texas, and the photo was taken at an angle that gave a good view of them. It wasn't always the face that identified the people. Body language was important, too. This picture at least gave a hint of how they stood.

Okay, then. He shoved his phone into his pocket. He hadn't needed to stop and ask which room the Ferrens were in. He'd already checked with the hotel when he was on his way. Since he owned the place, there hadn't been a problem getting the information.

He'd wanted to pick them up at the airport in Yuma. That way he'd have more control over the situation and of them. That would be especially important if they turned out to be a disaster and he had to get rid of them. At this point, he was ready to cross any lines to be sure the events of the target date succeeded. The couple had insisted, however, on having their own vehicle. Jed could understand that. He'd feel the same way. He just hoped there wasn't some underlying reason that he'd yet to find out about. Like what? he asked himself as he waited for the elevator. He hoped he was just being careful and not paranoid.

He stepped into the elevator that whisked him smoothly to the top floor where the suites were located. He turned right and walked to the door at the end of the hall, the carpet so thick his steps were soundless. He paused a moment then rang the bell embedded in the molding. That had been his own suggestion, a nice touch, he'd thought, for people paying top dollar for these accommodations.

The door was opened by a tall, lean man whose dark hair and beard were sprinkled with silver. There was no missing the confidence he exuded or the *you can kiss my ass* attitude. A man who had seen and done it all. He was a little older than the pictures Jed had seen. There was no mistaking, however, that he was Bernardo's brother. He had the same aura of confidence, that of someone who has made an unseemly large fortune doing a lot of things that weren't quite legal and getting away with it.

Don't fuck with me

The man might as well have been wearing a T-shirt with the statement. For a moment, Jed wondered who was the real brains behind Ferren Arms and if Max should have been the one they tapped. For the first time, he felt a little uneasy about interrogating this man, no matter how politely he did it.

Max smiled, showing even, white teeth. "You must be Jed." He held out his hand. "Max Ferren. Come on in."

Jed stepped into the suite's living room and shook Max's hand. The handshake was as firm as he expected.

"A pleasure meeting you." At least Jed hoped it was.

"And this is my wife, Regan."

Jed turned to the woman who rose from the couch. He had only seen a few pictures of her but, again, as with Max, there was nothing in her appearance to set off warning bells. She obviously took excellent care of herself, her auburn hair falling in lustrous waves to her shoulders, her skin nearly flawless and perfectly made up. The dark slacks and silk blouse she wore draped nicely over a toned, mature figure. When he shook her hand, it was warm and smooth, and, he noted, skillfully extracted from his grip. If he were given to making passes at other men's wives— Wait! He was! But. Not within this little group. That would be like playing with dynamite.

"A pleasure to meet you," he told her then looked from one to the other. "I understand this marriage is recent?"

"It is." Max nodded. "I waited a long time for the right woman."

"I'm happy to see you've found her. Congratulations to both of you."

Regan gestured to a tray on the coffee table holding a carafe, cups, and a plate of miniature pastries. "I took the liberty of ordering something. I find having conversations over coffee always makes them go so much more smoothly. Please have a seat and let me fill a cup for you."

Her voice was a warm contralto, soothing yet at the same time confident. Not a woman Jed would want to cross. He found it interesting that she not Max, seemed to take the lead in this situation, but maybe that was by design.

When everyone was seated—Max and Regan on one couch, Jed on the other facing them—Regan gave him a smile that felt strangely as if it had skewered him.

“I understand how unsettling it has to be for all of you,” she told him, “to have this switch take place at what is a critical time. I’m sure it’s made you all question the situation.”

“I’m not—” he began.

“Please be assured,” she interrupted, “that Bernardo has fully briefed us on everything. Also, Max works very closely with his brother at Ferren Arms Manufacturing and can deliver on what is needed. We’re happy to answer any questions you have to put your mind at ease. But understand, we also have some questions of our own.”

“Of course, and I’ll be happy to answer them. Bernardo said he made you aware of the critical nature of this meeting and the timeline.”

“He did.” Max nodded. “Although he and I had been discussing it a lot recently. We wanted to make sure you were ‘sufficiently supplied.’”

Jed nearly smiled. Sufficiently supplied was a mild way of putting what their needs were.

“Fine. Then let’s get to it, shall we? The others in our group have some concerns regarding your readiness that I promised to address, and I, of course, will answer yours.”

“The meeting starts in two days,” Regan pointed

out. "Did you really think you needed that much time to assure yourself we're the real deal?"

Jed shifted in his seat. These were not novices or also-rans as Lorena and Gavin had feared. They were very smart people. Max might even be smarter than his brother. And Regan? In just the few minutes since he'd arrived, he'd realized there was more depth there than any of them had expected. He wasn't just the shadow of his brother that they'd feared, even tried to prepare for. His earlier thoughts popped into his brain, and he wondered why the hell these two people weren't at the helm of Ferren Arms Manufacturing.

When they were all settled with their coffee, Jed cleared his throat.

"I thought it might be good for all of us if we reviewed the situation before the meeting starts tomorrow. Just, you know, to make sure you were up to speed." He pulled out his patented friendly smile. "I know your brother has kept you in the loop from the beginning. He said—"

"Every decision that impacts Ferrens Arms is made together," Max interrupted.

He didn't sound angry or pissed off. No, there was something more dangerous there Jed was almost looking forward to Max and Lorena meeting for the first time.

Now he just nodded. “We’re all well aware of that, but please look at it from our perspective. We have a deadline looming in front of us, and we need something more than Bernardo’s assurance that you can step in without causing a hiccup.”

“So this little meeting isn’t just to be sure we have all the information we need, right?” Max’s smile made winter look warm. “No problem. I’d do the same thing in your situation. Bernardo told us it would be on the agenda, so fire away.”

Jed had a format for the afternoon, and he was determined to stick to it, but he couldn’t shake the feeling that he was the one being dissected. His very brief moments with Max Ferren during the years hadn’t shown him this side of the man at all. Why hadn’t Bernardo warned him about his brother and sister-in-law? Of course, what would he say? Watch out for them? On the surface they were friendly, smart, and cordial. Yet he kept getting the feeling they were just tolerating him, and he didn’t like it one bit.

By the time the afternoon ended, he felt as if he was the one being subtly interrogated. He’d told the others he’d be spending two days at this, but, truth be told, he didn’t think he had much more to ask. It would be up to the others to judge now. He drained a last cup of coffee and rose from the couch.

"I want to thank you for going through all of this with me. It will help to be prepared when you get to the lodge." He pulled out his public smile. "Hope I wasn't too much of a pain."

"Not at all," Regan said. "As Max told you in the beginning, we have some questions of our own that we hoped to ask."

"Then how about meeting my wife and myself for dinner tonight, as our guests? I had planned on extending the invitation anyway."

The couple exchanged glances then Regan nodded.

"That would be incredibly nice of you. The plans in place will completely change the face of this nation. We wouldn't want to do anything to screw it up."

"I'm sure that's not even possible," Jed told them. "Bernardo would not have sent you in his place if it was. So how about if I give you some time to yourselves and pick you up about seven. That work?"

"Not necessary," Max told hm. "Just tell us where to meet you."

Yes, Jed thought, these are people who always want to control their situation. The meeting at the lodge was going to be interesting.

"Works for me."

They decided on a restaurant and a time, they all shook hands, and Jed left the suite. As he headed for the elevator, he breathed a sigh of relief. He felt completely wrung out, yet the Ferrens had still looked cool and collected when they were finished. There was something here, something he could not put his finger on, which was unusual for him. Maybe when they threw their questions at him tonight, he'd figure it out. He just wasn't happy with the feeling the dynamics of the group were about to change, and maybe not for the better.

He had silenced his cell when he entered the suite, but now he pulled it from his pocket and checked the call log. Six from Lorena plus several from each of the others. Figured. Damn! It amazed him how people with ice in their veins, who plotted mass murder without shedding a drop of sweat, who planned the destruction and takeover of a government, could be thrown off-kilter by something like this. Yes, this was a crucial situation but there were options. If Bernardo's in-laws proved unstable or uncertain, he'd just arrange to have them taken care of. He'd force Bernardo to handle their supplies even if it killed him in the end, and they could move forward with their plans.

He'd said he'd take care of things and get back to them. They'd known he'd be tied up all afternoon. He hit redial for Lorena first.

"Well?" she answered.

Jed smiled to himself. This conversation was actually going to be a pleasure.

"You have no worries," he told her.

"And what do you base that on?" she demanded. "Did your meeting with them go that well?"

"Better than I expected." He paused, choosing his next words carefully. "First of all, they match the photo I had of them, as much as anyone can match pictures taken of them. Second, these people are not here just because they are Bernardo's relatives. In fact, I'm beginning to wish I had spent more time with Max over the years. I might have extended the invite to him instead."

Silence. Then, "Explain, please."

Jed chose his next words carefully. "I have a funny feeling that Max is actually the one running the company, or at least handling all the backroom deals. He's not someone I'd want to get on the bad side of. And I have a feeling he'll have some ideas to tighten up our plans."

"I don't want a stranger coming in and fucking things up," she snapped.

"Lorena." He made his voice as calm and even as possible. "I know you think you know more about what needs to be done than anyone, but you'd do well to listen to these people."

"We are three weeks away from kickoff," she reminded him. "Tinkering with things now would be a big mistake. And I know you don't like to make mistakes."

"Nor do I make them." His fingers tightened on the phone.

There was a long pause. "If you vouch for them, I'll listen to what they say. That's all I'll commit to right now."

"Fair enough. I'm going to call the others then I'm going to meet Max and Regan for dinner. I'll text everyone after that."

He disconnected without waiting for her to hang up. After this upcoming meeting, next on his agenda was figuring a way to contain Lorena Alvaro without shutting off her connections. Once they made their move, they'd still need the cartel for a number of things. He couldn't shut off that faucet, especially since they had contacts all over the world.

When valet parking brought his car, he pulled away from the hotel and drove down the street to a strip center. He pulled into a space in the back, took out his cell again, and began to call the other partners.

*****

Max tore a sheet of paper off the notepad by the telephone in the living room, flattened the paper on the coffee table, and wrote a short note.

Normal conversation. Suggest we get a drink downstairs.

Regan nodded.

"I thought this was a good beginning for us with this group," she said in an even tone. "Don't you agree?"

"I do. Jed Whitlow seems to have his act together, and Bernardo told us the others were the same. I'm looking forward to this meeting at the lodge."

"Yes. I'm anxious to hear the final details of the plan." She studied his face, watching for clues as to what to say next.

"We have a little time before we have to meet Jed for dinner. How about a drink downstairs?"

"Sounds good to me. We can leave right from the bar."

The first thing Max had done when they arrived at

their suite was to check every inch of the place for listening devices. Jed Whitlow owned the hotel, he wasn't too happy with this substitution, and they fully expected he'd bug every inch of the place. Si had given him a sophisticated piece of equipment that could locate anything, and, sure enough, they'd found seven of them scattered in the living room and bedroom. The bathroom seemed to be the only place they'd have any privacy.

He motioned with his hand for her to keep talking.

"Let me just get my things, and I'm ready."

"Great."

Max stuffed his cell phone as well as the tiny electronic detecting gadget in his pocket then opened the door for her. They took the elevator downstairs and went into the bar located just off the lobby. Max guided her to a table in a far corner. Even though they thought it might be impossible, he pulled out this little gadget and took a slow stroll around the room, checking for listening devices anyway. At last, Max put away the device and sat down.

"We're all clear. Let's order our drinks."

"You really think he'd bug the bar?" Regan asked in a low voice.

"He owns the hotel," Max reminded her. "No

telling what he'd do. And there are probably people staying here now and then whose conversations he really wants to listen in on."

"What a way to live," she commented, her voice still pitched low.

They ordered their drinks and made small talk until the waiter served them and moved away.

Max took a swallow of his and set the glass down. "So what did you think of this afternoon?"

"You first," Regan said. "Impressions, please."

A woman who likes to be in control, Max thought. But not in an offensive way. She had a quiet strength and a sense of self-worth he didn't find very often in women. Except maybe in those his friends had been lucky enough to marry. Maybe he'd been looking in the wrong places. No, he hadn't been looking for quality at all, except in bed. And what did that say about him? All these years he'd been trying to convince himself he couldn't give everything to the SEALs and still have anything left over for a relationship. That his friends who married were the exception rather than the rule. Now he wondered if Fate had been saving him for Regan Shaw? And if so, would she be pleased or threaten to cut off his balls? More importantly, would she think he was nuts for having these feelings in the middle of an op that meant the future of the United States?

Hell! He probably was. He just couldn't win. Anyway, he was a SEAL first, and he needed to remember that. But he should at least put her on notice, in case he behaved in a weird way.

Weird. Yeah. God, Max.

"Max?" Regan's voice cut into his thoughts. "Did you go somewhere without me?

"No, just thinking." He took another swallow of his drink. "I've met too many men like Jed Whitlow in my lifetime. Too much money gives him too much power, makes him think he's unstoppable. Reminds me of some of the warlords we took down in the sandbox. Men like that are dangerous because they wield their power with the force of their egos."

"I got the same impression," she agreed. "He didn't seem too anxious to give us any more details than he thought we'd learned from Bernardo. He just kept saying it would be better for us to get the rest all at once along with the updates."

"I wonder who's controlling the flow of information and how close to the vest he—or she—let's not forget Lorena Alvaro—is playing it."

"A very good question," she agreed. "And did you

notice those little questions he kept sliding in? Questions I'm sure he thought would trick us. Catch us off guard."

Max nodded. "I'm pretty sure he wasn't prepared for two people slicker than he was. But if nothing else, he knows we aren't idiots or pushovers."

"He could also think we're dangerous to him," Regan pointed out. "It's obvious he's a man who likes to control things, and we already know Lorena Alvaro is pushing his buttons. I can't wait to sit at the table with him. With all of them."

"I'm surprised Bernardo didn't have much more information than the target date. Along, of course, with the materials he was supplying and what the ultimate goal is."

"That one is enough to scare the crap out of me." He took a swallow of his drink. "I'd bet my next fresh catch he knows a hell of a lot more than he's given us but thinks playing dumb is his best bet. I need to mention that to Si."

"He's already there." Regan laughed. "Bernardo Ferren has no idea who he's dealing with. Si isn't going to leave him alone. Except to go to the bathroom. He's got two of his best men guarding Bernardo and 'coaxing' more information out of him."

A corner of Max's mouth hitched. "Of course he does. I wouldn't expect any less."

"We both have met too many people just like Jed Whitlow and I'm sure, based on Si's profiles, the others in this group are the same." She reached out and paced a slim hand on his wrist. "Analyzing is my business, Max. We'll be in control. Just remember that." She grinned. "As long as we stay alive."

"Yeah. Not funny, Regan."

"I know. But we can use a little levity right now."

Speaking in low tones, they sipped their drinks and continued to dissect the rest of the conversation with Jed. To anyone observing them, they looked like any other man and woman having a pleasant drink together.

"Well, I think we've dissected this body as much as we can," Regan teased. "We left hardly any flesh on it."

"I'd like to take the flesh off all of them," Max growled. "I never can figure out how people with obscene amounts of money can turn on the countries that allowed them to make that money in the first place."

"Power," Regan told him. "I have an acquaintance I used to have this argument with all the time. Put three little kids in a sandbox I used to tell her. It's a great sandbox, painted and with the finest white sand. Give them each an equal number of toys and tell them they can swap if they want, but they must share. In fifteen minutes, you have one kid hogging most of the toys and ordering the other two kids around."

"That's the damn truth," he agreed. He drained his glass, set it down in front of him, and leaned across the table so his face was closer to Regan's. Might as well put it out there and get past it. If this was a problem, they should deal with it now.

"You know, Regan, in all my SEAL training, one of the things I learned over and over again was the mission requires personal discipline. No matter how tough the assignment, no matter what my personal feelings might be, the mission was the only important thing. Everything else was sublimated to it."

"I know that." She smiled. "I was married to a SEAL, remember? And I work with several. Is there a problem I'm not aware of?" The smile disappeared from her face. "Is it me? Did I do something? I thought—"

He held up a hand.

"There isn't a thing wrong with you, Regan. You're not the problem. I am."

Regan frowned. "I don't understand."

He sighed. “I shouldn’t even be telling you this, but I thought you should know in case my behavior is odd at times. And just so you know, this is not a situation I’ve had to deal with before.”

“Damn it, Max. Whatever bug you’ve got up your ass, just spit it out.”

“Look.” He took in a breath and let it out. He was in very unfamiliar territory here. “We’re supposed to be acting like a couple who are for all intents and purposes newlyweds. I believe Si said they’d only gotten married less than a year ago.”

Regan nodded. “That’s correct.”

“That means we’ll be expected to project an air of intimacy. That’s not the hitch here. Damn it, Regan, I’m attracted to you. Have been since the first moment I laid eyes on you. And I don’t mean just the ‘Hey, I want to get in your pants’ kind of attraction.”

He stopped, trying to organize his words, and raked his fingers through his hair. This wasn’t just unfamiliar territory. It was damned embarrassing.

“Max, listen, I—”

He held up his hand. “Please let me finish. This is embarrassing enough as it is. I’m only telling you this because I’m trying to be a gentleman.”

“And you are,” she assured him, grinning. “A

perfect gentleman."

"Yeah, maybe not so perfect. I'm going to be working real hard to make sure this stays as playacting because it seems I'm...attracted to you."

A tiny smile teased at her lips. "Attracted? To me?"

"Yeah." He cleared his throat. "And think about it. To carry out this charade, we'll also be sleeping in the same room once we get to the lodge where the meeting's being held. My mind might be 100 percent on the business at hand, but I'm not sure my body is." He sighed. "Like I said, I unexpectedly find myself very attracted to you. No, more than just attraction. And it shocks the hell out of me. In my entire life, I've never had more than a superficial relationship with any woman. Never wanted one. Maybe that's why I'm so ripe for it, but I think it's way more than just that."

Her laugh was soft and musical and, when he looked across the table, he was surprised to see a faint blush color her skin.

"If you're saying what I think you are," she said slowly, "should I tell you I might be having the same problem?"

"Oh?" His eyebrows rose. "Is that a fact?"

She nodded. "I was actually counting on you and

your SEAL discipline to keep us both in line." She lowered her gaze. "Max, there haven't been very many men since Dylan. No one who really appealed to me that way. The few times I tried, it was a disaster for both of us. I just figured I'd be celibate for the rest of my life. Talk about being shocked at my body's reaction to you—that's a mild way to describe it. And I guarantee you have more experience with this than I do.

"But not the right kind." He took one of her hands in his. "Nothing's ever going to happen unless you want it to. I just thought you ought to be aware of this in case I do or say something by accident."

She gave a low, throaty laugh. "By accident? Huh. Too bad it wouldn't be on purpose." Then she leaned toward him. "Listen, Max. This may sound corny, but the future and safety of this country—maybe other countries—depends on you and I being able to put a stop to this and gathering information to put these people in prison. We're going to do just that."

"Yes, we are, despite my misbehaving libido."

"Max. You know your SEAL discipline will take control. You're an honorable man which is why you felt compelled to warn me your behavior might be a bit strange now and then and told me why. But if something happens between us, in the early morning hours, before we become the Ferrens again, well…" She shrugged. "I don't shoot friendlies."

He felt the tension easing from his body. "I'll do my SEAL best to keep a lid on it. But it's nice to know if the lid slips, you won't take my head off."

"How can I when I feel the same way. When this is over…"

"When this is over my engine will be revving full tilt. Now, let's get out of here and put on our pretend faces. Jed was so stunned that we weren't what he expected, maybe he will let a few things slip."

"Let's hope so. I was surprised that a man like him could be shocked by anything."

"Me, too." He raised his hand to signal for the waiter. "You ready, Mrs. Ferren?"

"As ready as I'll ever be, Mr. Ferren."

"Then, let's do it."

Chapter Six

Lorena Alvaro looked from her husband, Elias, to the man sitting next to him on the couch. A man she neither liked nor trusted but was tied to by an arrangement worth millions. An arrangement that was also about to open the door for more millions and untold power. If only he wasn't so obnoxiously arrogant and had more concern for other people. Of course, if that was the case, he wouldn't be where he was now.

Luis Rojas—known as *El Toro* because he was built like a bull—was one of the most powerful cartel leaders in Mexico. Maybe in all of Central America. He and Elias's brother had been friends since they were both *halcones* (falcons) in the cartel named for Luis's family. Now Luis was the leader of the group that rivaled Sinaloa and was continuing to expand its reach. They were among the most feared *narcotrafficantes* and considered the most adept at bringing high-value humans over the border.

More than a year ago, Elias's health had prompted him to remove himself from an active role and stick to his ranching. However, he hadn't removed himself from the arena altogether. He and Lorena received substantial amounts of cash for providing a sheltered route for both drug shipments and human cargo. Those high on the terrorist watch list who needed to leave their own countries and find a fresh base knew Rojas could bring them over safely and help them find places to recreate their terror groups.

However, as Lorena was fond of pointing out, one man's terrorist was another man's key leader. It was she and Luis who had first hatched the idea of using these terrorists to their advantage. They could wreak incredible havoc on Rojas's rivals, and the cartel's hands would be clean.

Then they had met the others—the Whitlows, the Emerys, the Cavanaughs, and the Ferrens—at a ranching convention, and they had all gravitated to each other. They all, it appeared, had seemingly unresolvable problems with the government and its regulations regarding cattle ranching. Jed had been the one to suggest they use one of the private dining rooms at the hotel for their dinner. They were heavily into expressing their resentment at the government restriction on land and water that adversely affected ranchers, and things had just unrolled from there.

Bernardo's heart attack had sent a wave of panic through everyone except Jed. Luis, although not at the table per se, had voiced the greatest misgivings.

"We all have a lot riding on this," he said now. "I don't like strangers showing up at the last moment like this. How do we know they really are who they say they are?"

Lorena nodded. “Neither do I, but Bernardo’s heart attack has been verified and his brother and sister-in-law vetted, using everything short of blood tests.”

“Maybe we should have included that,” Luis mused. “If anything goes wrong, the effect would be disastrous for all of us.”

“Luis.” Lorena sighed. “I know how you feel, but I promise you this. When we get to the lodge, if anything about this couple feels off, we’ll just isolate and detain them until the big day.”

“And how will that help?” Rojas demanded. “They’d still be alive and able to do damage to us after they’re released.”

“By then it won’t matter,” she pointed out. “We’ll be in control of everything, and our person will be in place as the head of the government. What possible damage could they do at that point?”

“I don’t like to speculate, but there are unlimited possibilities. I think it’s brilliant that you picked July 4th to do this. It will make the biggest impact.”

“Thank you. That’s what we thought.”

“But keep this in mind. After the initial event, the people in the government and the military who are not under our control will have a chance to regroup and plan. Believe me, Lorena, I know what I'm talking about. We've had agencies of this government using every possible trick to fracture and destroy my organization as well as other cartels. They don't give up."

"But this time we've planned for everything," she reminded him. "We've been very careful to set things up so no one yet knows who we are, and they won't until the appropriate time. We've chosen someone to be the face of our organization. He's just so happy to be sitting on the throne he doesn't care if we make all the decisions. The right people will be in place to make sure that's exactly what happens. Which is a good thing because by himself he's a disaster."

Luis took a cigar from his breast pocket, clipped the end, and pulled out his lighter. Lorena had a hard and fast rule about smoking in the house, but neither she nor Elias ever told Luis he couldn't indulge in his cigars. They'd learned a long time ago just which things they could push him on, and cigar smoking wasn't one of them. He lit up, took a heavy draw, and blew out a thin stream of smoke. "Just so you are aware, I'm doing my own investigating of this Max and Regan Ferren couple. I don't like surprises. They are seldom pleasant ones."

Lorena exchanged a look with her husband. Elias had said very little during this conversation. He always preferred she did the talking while he listened and analyzed. They both knew from experience that Luis had a habit of being heavy-handed with things like this, convinced no one would object to anything he did.

"Luis, we've known each other a long time. We've been honest with you about this from the beginning. Are you saying now you don't trust our information?"

"I'm saying that I have found it's always better to vet things for yourself." He glanced from one to the other. "You wanted our 'soldiers' as support for this. Our army, since you can't exactly tap your own military. We're providing the manpower to supplement what the terrorist leaders have gathered. We've been sending them all over your country to meet with the people you've put in charge so there will be enough manpower at every location."

To make sure they have enough on what they'd come to think of as E-Day for Explosion Day, Lorena thought.

"It would be foolish on my part," Luis continued, "not to investigate every possible thing that could go wrong. *Comprende?*"

"Yes, yes, yes." She flipped her hand in the air.

"But if you find something, anything at all, you come to us—to me—immediately. Do not act on your own. If you do anything to trigger something that blows up our plans..."

Luis held up a hand. "I am not about to affect that. I have as much at stake as you do."

That was almost true, Lorena thought. With a new structure for this country in place, the man would be free to expand his cartel operations in any area he chose. And the other cartels with whom he constantly fought for control of certain areas would have to take a back seat. That's just the way it would be set up. She knew he was aware of that and wouldn't be in a hurry to make a mess of it.

"I just ask that you be careful," she told him again. "Jed Whitlow met with the Ferrens all afternoon today, and tonight he and Anna are taking them to dinner. He didn't express any misgivings about them, so where is this coming from?"

Luis blew another stream of smoke and looked at her through it as it evaporated.

"Forgive me, senora, but Jed Whitlow cannot see through his own ego. It is convenient to let him believe he is the leader of the group. He does most of the work, and he is the conduit to provide the firepower. But once everything is in place, we may find it better to have someone else in charge."

"Like you?" Lorena gave an unladylike snort. "That will never happen, and you know it."

"No, my dear. I was thinking of you. With me as your silent partner. I cannot, obviously, be the face of this organization." His lips curved in a humorless smile. "Just the actual *el jefe*."

"They'll never approve it," she told him, even as her heart beat just a little faster. "Everyone in that group believes he should be the one at the head of the table. None of them will give up even an inch of their power."

She'd lusted for this since the beginning, knowing even then it would be an uphill battle.

"Then it's up to you to convince them." He drew another slow puff on the cigar. "Or you and I."

Lorena swallowed a sigh. Luis brought things to the table that none of the others could. They knew it, although admitting it was another matter. She'd have to count on the fact that they all wanted their plan to succeed so much that they'd acquiesce to *El Toro's* request.

"I will talk to them," she promised.

"Do it at this meeting," he insisted. "We're just

days away from the big event. As I said, I have sent many men to supplement the ones your imported rabble rousers have gathered together. This will ensure success. If I pull out..." He shrugged and blew a thin stream of smoke.

Lorena ground her teeth. They all knew just how disastrous that would be. She hated when Luis played this card, which he seemed to be doing more and more often lately.

"Please don't push me on this. It's enough juggling these egos to put the plan in motion and project what comes next."

"Just as long as you don't take too long."

"I will take care of it," she promised. "Remember though. We can't be sure, no matter what he says, how completely Bernardo Ferren briefed his brother. This will take some maneuvering if I am to be assured of his vote and that of his wife. And what if he's really on the opposite side of the fence? What if he's opposed to what Bernardo is involved in and is coming to this meeting to gather information to destroy us?"

Luis sorted a laugh. "Always suspicious, senora."

"As are you, I might point out. And it's how I've stayed alive and prospered all these years. Do you have any objections?"

"I leave it in your very capable hands, senora. Except for one thing."

She lifted an eyebrow. "What's that?"

"I still have an itch about this unfortunate last-minute substitution. I might take a little trip to visit Bernardo in the hospital myself. Just to be sure these people aren't spies."

"Spies?" She stared at them. "How would they even have learned about us? Luis, you're seeing shadows where there are none."

"That is how I've stayed alive and out of prison all these years. So I'm going to do a little investigating on my own. Be sure you have your cell phone with you at all times."

"Don't I always?" She sighed. "I have to admit I've wondered about this myself. Ferren wasn't one of the original group when we met at the cattlemen's convention. There were four couples in that dining room, discussing government over-regulation of resources that affect us as ranchers. Jed Whitlow brought Bernardo Ferren in as a source for weapons we could trust." She barked a laugh. "It wasn't as if we could look up someone online and place an order."

"I understand. Truly. But the rest of us only know what Whitlow has told us and what's available online.

And this last-minute substitution business gives me chills. I don't like the fact new people have been introduced at the last minute any more than you do. Like you, I also am a naturally suspicious person. I'm sure you don't mind if I do my own investigating." His lips curved in another of those humorless smiles she hated so much. "I have to check this situation out for myself."

Lorena was silent for a long moment, delicately gnawing her bottom lip.

"Fine. I agree with you. But if this is all legitimate, do *not* do anything to upset the applecart. If the Ferrens get pissed off and pull the deal for weapons, we have a huge problem."

Rojas tipped his head. "Understood. I will be careful and delicate and let you know what I find."

"As long as you don't do anything to screw this up," she warned. "And I want to be informed the minute you find anything. Assuming, that is, there's anything left to find."

"Of course."

Elias, who had been unusually silent throughout the conversation, cleared his throat.

"Lorena, Luis is not going to do anything that would disrupt the chance to make us even richer and more powerful." He turned to look at *El Toro*. "After all, this means broad international expansion for you, also. Am I right?"

"Of course. Of course."

"And we wouldn't want anything to happen to our relationship that spans generations. I'm right there, also."

Lorena thought how many people had begun to take her husband for granted when he fell ill. Luis had not been one of them and she knew his respect for the man had not wavered. It was one of the many reasons their business relationship continued to flourish.

Luis nodded.

"Excellent." She rose from her chair. "Then let me check with the cook. I believe dinner is almost ready."

But all she could think of as she headed to the kitchen was, *If that fucking bastard screws this up, I will kill him myself.*

*****

Silas leaned back in his desk chair and rubbed his eyes with the heels of his palms. His hands felt gritty and dry and no wonder, the amount of time he'd spent looking at the damn screen this afternoon. Normally, he'd assign this kind of research to someone who did it as part of their job, but it was important that he read every bit of the information himself to pick up any nuances. So many times you had to read between the lines.

Luis Rojas could win an award as one of the most evil men in the world. He had grown up as a foot soldier in the violent La Regla cartel, *regla* for rulers, which they had fully intended to become, until the day he assumed the mantle of control. There were whispers in back rooms that Rojas had gotten the throne not because he was the heir apparent but because he had killed off the three men higher than he was in the ranks and the two who had been discussed as logical successors. In dark corners and back rooms they called him *asesino*. Killer.

Si was certain Rojas fostered those rumors himself. What better way to keep people in line than to let them believe if they strayed, a bullet would find them. Or maybe they'd be burned alive. There were rumors he'd even had rivals thrown into the alligator pond at the rear of his sprawling estate. No one was anxious to test that theory.

When Regan Shaw had picked up the chatter that he and the cabal were forming an unholy alliance, his blood actually chilled. Take one group of people with more money than was good for them, no conscience, and a thirst for worldwide power. Add in a list of the most evil terrorists and the most bloodthirsty cartel—which was saying something—and the possibilities were worse than the worst nightmare.

He was searching for clues as to how the whole had come together. It was easy enough to band the ranchers in a group. One of his researchers had easily found a meeting they'd all been at and gravitated toward each other. It was no secret they chafed at many of the government regulations. They'd traced Bernardo Ferren's connection to Jed Whitlow from their college days. Digging up the information on the man's illegal arms sales and offshore accounts hadn't been all that easy, but that's what Bone Frog had experts for. The sickening part had begun to develop when Regan Shaw picked up the chatter about the high-value terrorists being smuggled into the country. The whole combination frightened the crap out of him, and he didn't scare easily.

They needed eyes and ears in the middle of this thing, and convincing his boss he should recruit Max DiSalvo had been an easy sell. Not so much where Regan Shaw was concerned. There was hesitation about putting her in a dangerous situation She wasn't after all trained for anything like this.

But Si had made his case and now, finally, it was all coming together. According to Bernardo, who he'd managed to scare the crap out of, this was the final meeting before they made their move. The fact they'd scheduled it for July 4th, as far as Si was concerned, showed a total lack of respect for this country, but it would certainly get everyone's attention.

He glanced at his watch. Almost nine o'clock. By now, Max and Regan should be finished with their second day of Jed Whitlow trying to pick them apart and another dinner with Jed and his wife. The man ought to be calling him shortly.

Even as the thought popped into his mind, his secure cell phone rang.

Max opened with, "Well, we've been vetted six ways from Sunday." He went on, "I think he's happy with us. And thank you for Regan. I don't think Jed was expecting someone who very nicely looked down her nose at him."

Si laughed. "Yeah, she can do that."

"Tomorrow's the big day, and we're as ready as we'll ever be," Max told him.

"Watch yourself. As prepared as you are, you never know when something's about to go sideways.

I'm still nervous about this cartel connection. Luis Rojas is an insane wild card."

"Understood. We'll be alert for anything and everything."

"The most important thing," Si told him, "is not to do anything that raises anyone's hackles and causes Rojas to go off the deep end."

"He's not going to be at the meeting, right?" Max confirmed. "Whitlow didn't mention it."

"He's not an official member of this cabal," Si assured him. "His connection is through the Alvaros. But I'd be shocked if he hasn't found a place to set up not far away. If these people were to pull this off, it would open the door for him to control worldwide drug distribution."

Max whistled. "Damn!"

"Right. So if he thinks you might throw a monkey wrench into this, he's liable to go off the rails and... Well, I don't even want to speculate. Just watch your six. Yours and Regan's."

"Will do."

"Where are you now?"

"Out behind the hotel in a little alcove where no one can see me. I told you the whole suite is bugged except for the bathroom."

"Not surprising. Okay. Check in when you can."

"You got it."

As he rode back upstairs in the elevator, he wondered how he'd last another night on the living room couch with a raging hard-on he was doing his best to conceal from Regan. Well, he slept in worse situations before.

Chapter Seven

The living room was empty when he let himself into the suite. He wondered if Regan was getting ready for bed this early.

No. Don't think about that.

He walked over to the big window and stood looking out at the lights of the little town below them.

"All set for tomorrow?"

He had not heard Regan come up beside him, and her voice startled him. The carpet in the suite was so thick the sound of footsteps was almost nonexistent. When she touched her fingers to his arm, a powerful electric shock ran through him. The first time they'd touched, a handshake the day they met, the little tingles that surged along his arm had startled him but not given him a lot of worry. He was, after all, a healthy man with healthy appetites. He might not be as young as he once was but that didn't mean his desire had faded. He'd had to keep reminding himself this was not just a business arrangement. It was also an assignment he'd accepted with the fate of the country at stake, so no hanky-panky.

So what if they were pretending to be a married couple? That didn't mean they had to enjoy all the benefits of marriage. Right? But holy hell! He couldn't remember the last time a woman gave him a hard-on so painful and insistent that at times it made it difficult to walk. He felt like a horny teenager and couldn't figure out what to do about it.

Wouldn't intimacy add to their appearance as a married couple? At forty-eight, he had enough learned discipline that even if his cock didn't get the message, his brain did. He knew how to behave in a critical situation. He was pretty damn sure, after the conversation with Regan yesterday, she felt the same way, but how to approach it? How to accomplish it? Both the living room and bedroom had listening devices, which meant, if they indulged in sex, they'd need to stuff something in their mouths to be quiet.

But he really felt they needed something after the past two days, and before they headed to the lodge in the morning. Jed had taken up a good part of their day again today, on the pretext of learning more about Ferren Arms, asking him too often to be accidental how the weapons would be delivered and if he'd been able to get the other ordnance the group had requested.

Now, standing in the living room of the suite, he wondered what his friend would say if he knew about the growing feelings for this woman. Or had he already guessed?

"Max?" Regan's voice was soft, with just the right casual tone. "Want to go down to the bar before we hit the hay?"

Going to the bar was their code for leaving the suite to talk without being eavesdropped on.

What would she do if he said, *I'd rather go to bed with you*? He'd prepped for a lot of missions with the SEALs, missions that required him to use the skills he had drummed into him over and over again. He could hit a target on the run, take down a tango with only one hand, make himself nearly invisible in the dark, and control his breathing so nothing gave him away. He should be able to figure this out, right?

"So, what do you think?" she prompted.

He turned to face her, hoping the naked hunger he felt wasn't written all over his face. "I'm still thinking."

She stood on tiptoe to whisper in his ear. "So am I. And I see in your eyes the same thing I'm feeling. I know we're on a mission, and self-discipline is the first thing we need. But there's something happening between us. I don't know about you, but it shocks the hell out of me. What I do know is we ought to do something about it. If we show up tomorrow wearing sexual tension like a second skin, these people will spot it right away. They'll either think our marriage is in trouble or we're not married at all. Right?"

He blew out a breath and nodded. She was right. He stroked his fingers across her cheek, cupped her ear, and pressed his mouth to it.

"I'm thinking," he whispered.

"About what? Am I being too forward?"

He shook his head. "I'm thinking that I need a shower. And about how much more I'd enjoy it if you were in there with me."

He felt her cheek muscles move as she smiled.

"What a splendid idea."

He took his hand away and raised his head. "I'm thinking it would be good to turn in early. Tomorrow's going to be a busy day. Driving to the lodge. Meeting everyone. Finally getting all the details Bernardo was too sick to give us."

"Good idea. I'm for a hot shower."

"Sounds good. Me, too."

"Ladies first, then. Go on."

"Thanks."

Max followed Regan into the bedroom, watching

the saucy little wiggle she gave her butt. He was so hard and swollen just from anticipation that walking was difficult for him.

He wondered how they'd handle getting undressed. He didn't want them to just strip off their clothes and go at it like fuck buddies. In the bedroom, they stopped and stared at each other. He made himself wait for signals from Regan. Even if the situation wasn't ideal, he would do this with class.

He was stunned when she stood there a moment then grabbed the edges of her sweater and slowly drew it over her head. He sucked in his breath at the sight of her nicely rounded breasts cradled in the cups of a lacy purple bra. The dark nipples were temptingly visible through the cutouts in the lace.

He waited to see if she would continue or if he should take off a piece of clothing. But Regan just drew in a deep breath, let it out, and unzipped her slacks. She kicked off her shoes, eased the slacks down her legs, and toed them aside as she stepped out of them. Now she stood before him in nothing but the bra and matching purple panties.

She had the ripe figure of a woman, hips flaring, thighs nicely rounded. He had to bite the inside of his cheeks to maintain any control or, like a horny teenager, he would have come in his pants.

Slow, he cautioned himself. Take it slow.

His gaze traveled the length of her body, and when it reached her face again, he was stunned to see uncertainty in her eyes.

"I *really* haven't done this in a long time," she whispered. Even her smile was a little shaky.

Max swallowed against the sudden surge of emotion in his throat. He remembered to keep his voice too low to be picked up. "Then I'm really glad you waited for me, even if you didn't know I'd be the one."

He stepped forward, cupped her cheeks, and placed a slow, tender kiss on her mouth. Her lips tasted faintly of the cherry cola she'd had with dinner, and it was a pleasant taste.

Cherry cola? Who the hell drank cola anyway?

He licked the surface of her lips, teasing at the corners before very slowly easing his tongue inside. And oh god, the taste was like an elixir. He licked slowly, letting the flavor seep into his mouth. Regan reached up to place her hands on either side of his head and, when he eased back on the kiss, whispered against his lips.

"Bathroom." She mouthed the word. "They'll be listening for the water."

"You're right."

Taking Regan's hand and tugging her along behind him, he strode into the bathroom, slid back the solid glass pane of the shower door, and turned on the faucet full blast. He could adjust it once they were inside. Then he turned, brushed a kiss over her mouth, and stripped off his clothes. He was surprised he didn't pop the buttons on his shirt, as fast as he pulled it off. He kicked off his shoes and yanked his pants and boxer briefs down in one movement, being careful not to do damage to his rigid, protruding cock.

Then he turned back to Regan, who stood there with a look on her face that was half hopeful, half fearful. He trailed his fingers along the line of her jaw, down her neck, and across the plump tops of her breasts. "It's going to be fine. You have my word. You just have to promise not to laugh if I can't hold off for more than fifteen seconds."

"Believe me. Laughing is the last thing on my mind."

Max couldn't believe his hands were actually trembling when he cupped her breasts and abraded the nipples through the lace of the bra. Nor could he believe how hard they were already. Pinching them between thumb and forefinger, fabric and all, he squeezed and tugged and rolled them, loving the little gasps of pleasure from Regan's throat. Her eyes were closed, her head tilted back, and her upper body arched into his touch. Hungry to taste her without the barrier of cloth, he reached behind her, unsnapped the bra, and pulled it off. When he captured one naked nipple with his mouth and bit down gently, she moaned, a sexy little sound he felt all the way to his groin.

Cupping the other breast, he kneaded it as he continued to suck on the nipple, drawing the beaded tip deep into his mouth and grazing it with his teeth. Regan clutched at his upper arms, arching herself more fully up to him. He switched sides, wanting to taste the other breast just as much, but impatience to see and feel and touch and taste the rest of her roared through him.

Taking a step back, he ignored her little cry of protest and lifted her onto the bed, placing her right at the edge. He stripped off her panties, nearly ripping them in his haste, spread her thighs, and knelt between them. And nearly lost it completely. The lips of her sex were so pink, bordered by neatly trimmed hair a shade darker than the auburn on her head. Her flesh glistened with moisture that beckoned for his tongue.

He inhaled, letting the sharp sweetness of her essence fill his lungs before pressing the lips open with his thumbs. With one swipe of his tongue, he tasted her from top to bottom, reveling in it, lapping it again and again. Opening her wider, he slipped his tongue inside and swirled it around in the tight channel.

Regan was making those sexy little noises again, sounds that only served to make him hotter and harder. When he removed his tongue and slipped two fingers inside her, she cried out and thrust herself against him. God, she was so tight inside. It was obvious she hadn't had sex in a long time, and he just hoped his cock would fit without hurting her. He moved his fingers in and out, coaxing her response, wanting her to be prepared for when she took his cock.

The sounds she was making were driving him crazy, and his cock was sending him urgent messages. He reached for the famous SEAL discipline and focused only on giving Regan pleasure. In and out his fingers slid, slowly at first, making sure to hit her sweet spot each time. When her inner walls began to flutter, he captured her clit with his mouth and tugged on it. It only took another moment before her climax roared through her, inner muscles gripping his fingers, hips thrusting at him.

He rode her through it until the last tremor subsided.

"Okay?" he asked when her eyes opened.

"Better than good. I wasn't even sure I could do that anymore."

"Oh, babe, you more than did it. And I'm glad it was with me."

Then he slipped his fingers from the grasp of her body, and, with her eyes still on him, licked each of his fingers, one by one. He saw heat flare in her eyes and the pulse at the hollow of her throat flutter as she watched him.

"You taste damn good, Regan," he whispered in her ear. "I want a lot more of that, but if I don't get inside you in the next sixty seconds, I really will embarrass myself."

And that was no lie. He hadn't been this urgently horny in longer than he could remember. He was famous for his control, for his ability to take a long time pleasuring a woman before he took them both to orgasm. That wasn't happening this time. Regan unlocked things inside him he hadn't even realized were hidden, and his cock was demanding he acknowledge them.

In seconds, he had grabbed his wallet from his pants pocket, extracted a condom, and rolled it onto his swollen shaft. He lifted Regan, yanked the covers back on the bed, and arranged her so her head was on the pillows. Then he climbed between her thighs, opening her wide, and knelt so the head of his cock was poised just at her opening. He wrapped his fingers around the pulsing shaft, and, locking his eyes with hers, very slowly pushed inside.

Holymotherfucking shit!

He'd died and gone to paradise. That was the only reason for the incredible feeling that washed through him and made every one of his hormones do a happy dance. She was hot and wet and tight, ramping up his pulse rate and making him want to ride her as fast as possible to come inside her. He gritted his teeth, forcing himself to hold back as he began the slow in-and-out, thrust-and-retreat motion. He locked his gaze with hers, registering every response, every change of emotion.

"Look at me," he demanded. "Don't look away from me. See what I'm feeling."

She locked her gaze with his as he demanded. What he saw was a wealth of emotion as strong and as unexpected as his, all mixed with intense need and hunger. Holy shit! This was better than a ride to paradise. It was beyond heaven. In all these years, he'd never had sex with a woman and felt like this. Except this wasn't just sex. It was what he'd been looking for all his life, and he'd better be damn good at it.

He forced himself to set up a slow rhythm, in and out, back and forth. He held himself back with superhuman effort until he felt her perched just at the edge of climax. His cock filled her, thick and hot and incredibly hard. She wound her legs around him, locked her ankles at the base of his spine, and pulled him as tight to her body as he could get. He balanced on one arm while he slid the other hand between them, found her clit, and began rubbing it.

In mere seconds, he saw the expression on her face change and felt the pulsing begin inside her core. Her inner muscles gripped his cock, and he stopped holding back and drove into her harder and faster, setting up a rhythm that she matched. He felt the beginnings of his orgasm just as her inner muscles started to ripple around his shaft, and he drove into her one last time, hot and hard. One more forceful thrust, and they were riding that roller coaster together.

Spasms gripped them as his cock pulsated inside

her, her inner walls convulsing and milking him. He caught himself on his forearms, waiting for his breathing to even out, not sure whose heart pounded the loudest, his or Regan's. When the shudders subsided at last, Max brushed a kiss over her lips before nuzzling the crook of her neck. He was so thoroughly spent he wasn't sure he'd ever be able to move again.

For a very long moment neither of them spoke. Max was almost afraid to say anything and break the spell, for fear he'd misread her, and he was the only one for whom this had been almost a religious experience. Then she smiled at him, and his heart began to beat again.

"Not bad for an old couple," she joked.

"Not old," he corrected, "just wonderfully mature."

He hated to break the connection with her, but he needed to get rid of the condom and clean himself up. When he returned to the bedroom, she was still in the same spot and still smiling. Thank god for that.

He turned off the lamp on the nightstand, slid into bed beside Regan, and turned her so she was spooned against him. Then he banded an arm around her and cupped a warm breast with his hand. When she pushed back against him, he was afraid his cock was going to rise up and demand more, and, for the moment, he wasn't sure he had it in him. He had some things he wanted to say, but he was choosing his words carefully. He wanted to get this right and not fuck up the best thing to come into his life ever.

"I can smell your brain burning," she teased.

"Regan." He hugged her tighter against him then pulled a pillow over them to make their voices indistinguishable and spoke so softly nothing could pick up their words. "I just want to be sure you know that was the best sex I've ever had in my life, and we hardly even got started. If I had the energy, I'd haul you back into the shower."

She gave a soundless chuckle. "Either you've had pretty bad sex, or you have very low standards."

He squeezed her firm breast and put his lips close to her ear so he could whisper, "Neither one of those is true. I was so hot for you I couldn't have taken a minute longer than I did. And that is definitely a first for me. I've never had this instant connection with a woman, Regan. Ever. I don't want to fuck it up. I know we have to put it on hold while we work this assignment, but after..."

He was far from ready to say the *love* word yet, but, at forty-eight, it was time. And he'd found the woman he could feel that with.

She took so long before she said anything else, Max was almost afraid to hear what she had to say.

"I never thought I'd find anyone after Dylan," she said at last. "He was it for me. My everything. When he was killed, it nearly destroyed me. But all the work I've done since then I looked at as a way to honor his memory because I was sure that's all I'd have."

Max held his breath.

"But then I met you, and another door opened. I'm glad we made love tonight, Max. That's going to hold us when we walk into the lion's den tomorrow. We both know this mission comes before anything. If we can't stop it, nothing else matters. But I know we will. And when this is over..."

"When this is over, I'd love for you to come up to Maine with me. Check it out. Try it out. Who knows? You might like it better than D.C."

"If you're there, that's already a big plus."

"Okay, then."

He brushed her curls back from her cheek and placed a whisper of a kiss on her cheek. Then he closed his eyes. They'd need every bit of sleep when tomorrow came around.

Chapter Eight

Max couldn't remember the last time—if ever—he'd been so emotionally involved in sex. His connection with Regan was a revelation that he could actually have that kind of relationship. They made love again just before falling asleep, slower and very delicious, and all the more erotic because they couldn't allow themselves to make a sound. By now he knew much more than his body was involved.

But they had a job to do that came first. Thank god his engrained SEAL discipline would allow him to pack it in a mental closet until this was over. And extra thanks that Regan was on the same wavelength. The assignment took front and center. No question about it.

They also knew that while they'd be sharing a bed at the lodge, sex would be off their list of activities.

"You know the room we'll be given is going to be bugged," Max told her as they lay sated and quiet in the dark.

"No question about it," she agreed.

"All that time we spent with him and his wife still

didn't answer all his reservations. I wouldn't put it past him to kill us—or have us killed—if he gets too suspicious."

"But wouldn't he worry that we might, after all, be the real thing, and Bernardo Ferren wouldn't be too happy if his brother and sister-in-law were murdered?"

"I think he'd rather deal with that," Max told her, "than have a snake in their midst that could destroy all their plans. Think about this. If we can't stop them, there will be major attacks at five separate locations that will kill thousands of people and destroy property. The government will be turning itself inside out to find out who did this, wonder where there might be other attacks, and figure out how to prevent them."

"I wouldn't put it past these people to follow it up with a series of smaller attacks the next day," Regan agreed. "The government will be in chaos, terrorists can run around shooting people at will, and by the time the dust settles, these people will be in control and have their figurehead in place."

Max nodded. "All the more reason we have to get information to Si so DHS can begin to take precautions."

Even after all the time they'd just spent with him, Max still had the feeling Jed didn't completely trust them. Regan told him she agreed with him. She got the same sense of reservation. And while Anna Whitlow had been polite and charming, the vibes they got from her didn't make them feel warm and fuzzy. There was a cold arrogance about her that made them wonder who actually was the driving force in their marriage.

"I'm wondering if it's such a good idea to bring you into this," Max mused.

"Don't even try to leave me out," she warned. "I can help you analyze everything we learned, not to mention the fact that I'm a damn good shot if I need to be."

Max had to admit she was right. They'd spent some time on the range at the place where they had been staying, testing the Ferren weapons, and she'd actually amazed him with her skill.

They ate an early breakfast the next morning then checked out of the hotel and headed out of town. As they drove to the Whitlow place the next morning, Max called Lou Valenti, the county sheriff who was their contact if necessary. Max drove while Regan dialed the number of the man's private cell and put him on speakerphone so they could both talk.

"I got a call from Si this morning, also," Valenti told them. "He knows I can't exactly do drive-bys of the place, but I'm available twenty-four seven if needed. And he gave me the numbers of the two guys who are your backup."

"Hopefully," Max told him, "we can get in, get our information, and get out. But I've learned not to count on plans working out as expected."

"We'll text you whenever we text our guys to keep them up to date," Regan said. "But I'm also hoping we can pull this off without needing any of you and get the hell out of there."

"Take care of yourselves," Valenti said, "and keep me on speed dial."

Twenty minutes later they turned off the two-lane highway onto a gravel road that wound between thick stands of trees. Regan's eyes widened as they reached the end of the road where a house stood in the center of a large clearing. Beyond it stood two more smaller buildings. Calling this a lodge, she thought, would be too simple. It soared three stories toward the sky, with a wide front porch and large picture windows. The only thing rustic about it was the polished log exterior. Otherwise, even from a distance, she could tell no expense had been spared.

Acres of forested land stretched from all sides of the building. Talk about being isolated.

"This is certainly some place."

Max chuckled. "I'd only bring you to the nicest places."

"Must be nice to have money to waste on something like this," she told Max.

"Yeah, but I wouldn't change places with him for anything. What kind of man plots the overthrow of his country, anyway?"

"The kind who thinks his power is unlimited."

Max had parked in a large gravel area that already held several other vehicles.

"Looks like we're the last ones here," Regan commented.

"Good. That means we can meet them all at once and don't have to worry about getting caught up in conversations with each couple as they come in. One big blast is better."

"We might even be able to play them off against each other. Find out the locations of the strikes. They picked a symbolic day to do this. They'll want it to happen at the most visible sites."

"I hope they go over it early on. There are at least fifteen major celebrations that day. I know Si could arrange to have all of them covered, but it would be nice if he didn't have to."

"Agreed."

Regan sighed. "Well, I suppose we should get to it."

Now he turned to her and took her hand. "Before we go in and put on our costume faces, I just want to tell you how great last night was."

Heat burned her cheeks. "For me, too. I know I was out of practice, but—"

"You were just what I wanted," he told her in a low voice. "In every possible way. It centers me to be able to pull off this charade and be successful at it."

She squeezed his hand. "Me, too."

"When this is over..."

"Yes. When this is over."

"We should go in." Max released her hand with obvious reluctance. "Whitlow is probably pissed we didn't let him pick us up or at least follow him here. And I'm sure he's been watching for us from whatever screen the security system feeds into."

"Okay, let's go be the Ferrens and figure out how to pull the plug on this."

Max grabbed their suitcases as well as his briefcase out of the trunk of the car and followed Regan up to the house. Just as she was about to knock on the door, a tall, lanky man with graying curly hair pulled it open. She recognized him from the pictures she'd printed out.

"Come in, come in. Glad to see you found the place without any trouble." He stepped back and waved them inside. "Come on in and meet the others."

Max shook the proffered hand and nodded. "Good to see you again. Bernardo is grateful you're letting us fill in for him. He's very much invested in this, you know."

"I do know. He and I go back a long way. I was delighted when he agreed to come on board."

As if he just realized he'd cornered them in the doorway, Jed reached for one of the suitcases. "Here. Let me help you with these. Under normal circumstances, I'd have my caretaker haul them to your room. However, considering the nature of this meeting, I thought it best to give him a few days off."

"Good thought."

Jed took both suitcases and placed them to one side of the large foyer. Max held onto the briefcase, and Jed just shrugged. Regan would have bet a month's pay while they were occupied in the meeting, someone would be going through them looking for any evidence they were imposters. That was one reason why Max's weapons were in the hard-sided suitcase, locked in a special compartment invisible even to the most intrusive inspection. They had their special pens with them.

"This way, then. The others are already gathered around the table. Did you have breakfast? I've got a selection of pastries, but if—"

Regan held up her hand. "We're good. We ate before we checked out."

"Okay, then. Let's get you hooked up with everyone else."

He led them through the living room to a large dining room with huge windows on two sides. Sheer drapes covered the windows, cutting down the glare of the sun. Seven people were sitting at the table, coffee mugs in front of them along with plates of pastry that had no doubt come from the large tray in the center. They all looked at Max and Regan with a mixture of curiosity and hostility.

Jed made the introductions then indicated the two empty seats between the Cavanaughs and Whitlow's wife. The empty chair at the head of the table was obviously Jed's.

"So nice to see you again. Glad you found the place. Jed said he'd have been happy to pick you up, you know."

"That was so very kind and thoughtful of him." Regan could fake a smile with the best of them. "But we felt we'd already imposed enough. You know, dinner two nights in a row, and Jed spending all that time bringing us up to speed. I know we're last minute substitutions but really, we just need to learn the details of anything that happened since the last meeting, and we're good to go." She looked at Max. "Right, dear?"

He nodded in agreement.

"All right, then." Jed gestured at the setup on a credenza with a large coffeemaker and mugs. "Coffee?"

"Yes." Regan nodded. "Thanks."

She and Max carried full mugs to their seats then sat while Jed made the introductions. She wondered what everyone's reaction would be, but she didn't have long to wait.

Lorena Alvaro leaned forward in her seat, fixing both of them with a hard stare.

"I don't like to beat around the bush," she said. "Tell us why Bernardo thought you and your wife would be good substitutes in this situation. We want to be sure the two of you have the same commitment he and Jeanne have."

Regan swallowed a smile. She'd dealt with a lot of

women like Lorena over the years, but she waited to see what Max would say.

"We're very close ideologically," Max told her. "In fact, I know you're aware that he and I have been discussing this group ever since it was formed." He looked around the table. "Besides, he couldn't have made the arms commitments without me. We own the company equally."

Regan watched everyone's faces as Max spoke. The Cavanaughs might as well as have been wearing masks, their faces showing no emotions at all. The Emerys looked as if they were examining bugs under a microscopic lens. Lorena Alvaro's posture gave the impression she didn't like this last-minute change at all. Her husband simply stared at them. Only Anna Whitlow, who they'd had dinner with two nights in a row, had a smile of any kind for them, although Regan wasn't sure she'd call it welcoming, either.

"Bernardo was going to bring the final inventory on the arms and munitions," Gavin Emery said in his gravelly voice. "That was so we could review it and make sure we had enough."

Max nodded, lifted his briefcase to the table, opened it, and took out thin file folders. He also removed his pen from his pocket, and Regan retrieved hers from her purse. They were now good to go with audio and video. She just hoped the damn things really worked. They tested them several times at the house outside of D.C., but she knew better than most how easily electronics could fuck themselves up.

"This is the list Bernardo said you all agreed on at the last meeting," Max told them as he distributed the folders. "I've read it over. You outlined for him how many men would need to be armed and what the plan for each location was so we could gather the inventory. I understand there are still some final decisions to be made. So, just to be safe, he drew up a list for every one of the spots."

Each of the people seated there opened the folders and studied the contents.

Kurt Cavanaugh looked up from his first.

"Wait. Bernardo didn't give you a final list? That's not what this is?"

"How could it be when the locations have yet to be confirmed. I thought that's what part of this meeting was for."

Regan noticed all eyes focused on Max. This was the first big test. Bernardo Ferren had indeed told them that, but he could have been lying. It could have been a little nugget he planted that would show the others she and Max were ringers. She held her breath, waiting for someone to speak.

At last, Kurt nodded. "That's true. And it's very thorough of you and Bernardo to have prepared a list for each place."

"Bernardo is always thorough," Jed told them.

"I know I'm late to the actual party," Max said, "but if we're going to meet the deadline, I need to know those locations today. Guns and munitions don't just deliver themselves. Some of them we'll truck in, some we'll fly in on chartered planes. And we have to do it in a way that doesn't raise anyone's suspicions as we move them into place. But we have to have locations plus the number of people who will need to be armed."

"We also need to know," Regan put in, "how many people at each location will be handling the explosives and if they're familiar with them."

"Why don't we call Bernardo," Lorena said in a sharp voice. "We can get him in on this with a conference call. Then we can be doubly sure we have the right figures and correct information."

Max looked around the table, and, when he spoke, ice dripped from his voice.

"Perhaps Ferren Arms and Munitions is not the

right partner with you for this, after all." He looked at Jed Whitlow. "You and Bernardo have been friends for years. It's unfortunate that you and I never had much occasion to spend time with each other but, as I'm sure you know, my brother and I each have our own circle of friends. I can assure you he would not have sent me in his place if he did not think I knew what I was talking about." He closed his folder. "As I said before, maybe you need to contact someone else to handle this. Trust is very important. My brother became involved with you because he believes in what you are doing. But if you don't trust us, we have nothing more to say to each other." He pushed back his chair. "Come on, Regan. This has all been a fucking waste of our time."

Regan forced herself to appear calm, gathering the items in front of her while the people at the table absorbed what Max had just said. Si had discussed this with them and told them it might happen. And also that there could be more than one challenge until the people around this table were satisfied with Max's presence. If they let the two of them walk out without a word, the shit would hit the fan. There wasn't time to plant someone else in the group to get the details. And on top of that, they might just decide to kill her and

Max. Once E-Day, as they were calling it, took place, it wouldn't matter anymore.

Jed Whitlow was the first to crack a smile.

"That's exactly what your brother would have said." He looked around the table. "All right? Everyone satisfied that this man is who he says he is and that he is here with Bernardo's full faith and confidence? We need to get down to business."

Regan let herself relax in slow increments. Okay. They'd jumped the first hurdle, but she was sure it wasn't the last. These people had everything at stake. They were rolling the dice on the biggest gamble of their lives. If it worked, they'd control the entire United States and then, little by little, the rest of the world. They could not afford to make any mistakes.

She did her best to appear calm and businesslike for the rest of the morning as she listened to everyone at the table discussing the merits of the different locations. They had the same list Si had shown them of the fifteen largest Fourth of July celebrations in the States. Washington D.C. with the celebration on the Mall at the top of everyone's list. If this group was lucky, they'd also hit a lot of elected officials and politicians at this particular spot. Bone Frog had already figured that out. It was the other locations that needed to be identified.

Lorena Alvaro put down the sheet of paper she'd been studying and looked around the table. It was obvious in that marriage who the dominant partner was, Regan thought.

"Let's consider some other things here." She rose, refilled her coffee mug, and sat down again. "We want to spread it out across the country, so we should not focus completely on the East Coast."

Kurt Cavanaugh nodded. "Agreed. We want every area to feel the impact."

"Remember," Lorena continued, "that Luis will have men at each location to provide enough manpower. And if we pick sites where he already has working groups, that will give us a greater reach."

"By groups do you mean gangs?" Max asked, his voice deceptively mild.

She glared at him across the table. "Perhaps your brother did not explain this to you thoroughly, Senor Ferren, but Luis Rojas is our ace in the hole. He runs the second most powerful cartel in Mexico and South America. We are fortunate that he is committed to being part of our plan."

"No question about it." Max's voice was deceptively mild. "I'm simply trying to fix in my mind who plays what part and who the people are who will be carrying out these actions. I have every confidence that the men who work for Rojas will do exactly what they are supposed to."

"And more," she sniffed. "He's providing the bulk of the manpower to fire these weapons and set off the explosions. Doing it in a place where they already have a foothold and can then use the situation to consolidate their own power is a win/win situation for everyone."

"Okay, great." Max nodded. "I understand, and I have no desire to disrupt that. Just trying to maximize everything all the way around. My suggestion is we include Houston on the list. Texas is a key area, and it will make a huge impact there." He looked across the table at Lorena. "And I'm going to assume Rojas has a significant functioning organization in that region, also. Am I correct?"

"Yes." Lorena nodded. "He has a strong foothold in that region."

"I don't mean to usurp anyone's authority here." He glanced at Jed Whitlow. "As I understand from Bernardo, you are, in fact, the unofficial chairman of this group."

"I am. Although we are all equals here, it works

much better when things funnel through one person."

"Of course. I was just going to note that we should get photographs of the venues where each event is held so we can pick the best locations to station the shooters and place the explosives for maximum effect."

"We also need shots of the past two years," Gavin Emery added, "so we can see where they station the cops and if the setup changes."

"And don't forget the snipers they station on the roofs," Regan added, playing her part as she'd been instructed. She looked around the table and saw that everyone was staring at her. "I've been to enough celebrations like this to know they always have snipers stationed somewhere high up. Usually on the roof. Once you identify where they are, you need to figure out a way to get someone up there and take them out."

Jed cleared his throat. "Good point. We discussed that but thanks for reminding us."

His voice wasn't quite so hostile, and she noticed Anna Whitlow studying her with a different look in her eyes and swallowed a smile. Whatever these people had expected, it wasn't what they were getting.

As the morning progressed, they discussed the logistics of each remaining site, eliminating some. It amazed her how calmly they could sit here discussing plans to kill hundreds, maybe even thousands of people, as if they were writing a grocery list. She had to keep reminding herself these people had created a plan to take over the world in the same manner, with cold, calculating deliberation and with their handpicked person in the leadership seat.

She wondered if they'd get around to discussing that. And if she and Max would learn the name of the puppet they were setting up to be their front man.

By one o'clock they had settled on the rest of the locations—New York, New Orleans and, strangely, Columbus, Ohio.

"That's an odd one," she commented. "Not Boston, which might have a larger crowd?"

"We've already agreed on New York," Kurt Cavanaugh reminded her. "Columbus, surprisingly, has one of the largest celebrations, and we want to hit different areas of the country."

She nodded and looked at the map they'd each been handed. "Makes sense."

"On that note," Jed Whitlow said, "I'd say it's time for lunch. Tonight we'll barbecue," he told everyone, and glanced at Max and Regan. "The first night of these meetings we like to relax with a good meal and a glass of bourbon. Or whatever your alcohol of choice is."

"Sounds good to us," Max told him.

Anna Whitlow pushed back her chair and stood up. "As usual, we've had everything else catered. It will only take a few minutes to get it all on the table."

"I suggest you all stretch your legs," Jed told them. "Return any business calls you need to. Whatever. Give us fifteen minutes."

"I think we'll step out to the patio," Max said to no one in particular. "You all have been here before, but we'd love to look around."

"Help yourselves," Jed told them. "Just be careful of the wildlife and the snakes."

They can't be any worse than the snakes in this room, Regan thought.

"Thanks for the tip." Max nudged her arm. "You'll protect me, right?" He looked across the table at those still gathering their things together. "You'd never know it to look at her, but Regan's a crack shot."

Some of them gave her a startled look. Then Gavin Emery laughed.

"I always did like a woman who could shoot straight." It was the first humorous thing he'd said since the meeting began.

Regan just smiled. She wasn't about to mention

the fact that she and Max had spent an entire morning at the gun range where they were staying, working with Ferren firearms. She was, however, damn glad they'd done it. The Ferren version of the Glock, for example, was one of the best weapons she'd ever handled.

Happily, no one followed them outside, preferring instead to wander to other rooms in the house to conduct their business. They strolled to the end of the oversized patio and stood to one side, where they could see the landscape and also anyone exiting the house.

"It seems no one wants to be overheard," Max joked.

"I'm with them, but wow. For a group of people planning to take control of the world, they don't seem to have a lot of trust in each other."

"Goes with the territory. Meanwhile, we have to talk quickly," Max told her. "No telling when we might be interrupted."

"You think someone's gone through our luggage yet?"

He nodded. "Without a doubt. Probably one of Whitlow's security guards. He never travels without them and I'm sure they're making themselves scarce around here, at his orders. Ever wonder why a rancher needs security guards?"

"He'll tell you it has nothing to do with ranching and everything to do with his excessive fortune and the people always hounding him. I'm sure he's got a couple stashed away here. But they didn't find the concealed compartment, or we would have heard about it."

"It's nearly impossible to find," Max assured her. "But I need to get the luggage up to our room and at least get the small handguns out. I keep getting strange vibes from these people. I have a feeling they still don't trust us."

"Would you if you were them? If I was planning to overthrow a government, I'd be paranoid about every new face that came into my group, even if it had supposedly been vetted."

"True that. Listen, I have to contact Si and give him the names of those locations. Just in case something slips through and we can't stop everything, he'll need to have defenses in place."

"Go ahead. You have your secure cell. And thank god for that, or I'm sure they'd figure out a way to tap into it." She looked through the glass doors into the dining room. "I see others are using their phones, too, so you won't attract any undue notice."

He grinned at her. "My darling 'wife,' in case you

hadn't noticed, we are the icon of undue notice. Those people kept eying us as if we had the plague."

"I guess I can't blame them. I'd feel the same way in their situation." She glanced inside and back at Max. "I just hope to hell Si is able to keep all the real Ferrens under wraps until this is over."

"I have every confidence in the world he can do it." He paused. "Although things can go to shit without even a moment's notice."

"Yes, I know." Sadness filled her eyes. "That's what happened with Dylan's mission."

"Damn, Regan." Max rubbed the back of his neck. "I'm sorry, I—"

She held up a hand. "It's okay. I've learned to live with it. But it also taught me never to trust any situation. You'd better hurry and call Si before someone else wanders out here."

Max hit speed dial and turned away from the house to give a short report to Silas. Regan made a show of checking her phone for messages as she saw some of the others doing. She was glad when he finished his call.

"Okay, he's all over it," Max reported. "I told him I'd check in again after dinner."

"They haven't brought up Luis Rojas yet," she

reminded him. “I kept waiting for Lorena Alvaro to say something, but she didn’t and neither did anyone else.”

“Let’s see what they say this afternoon when I ask about manpower. And I’m trying to figure out a way to ask about what comes next without making them realize Bernardo didn’t give us a lot of details.”

“We’ll play it by ear the way we do everything else.”

“I’ve got the pen with the audio,” she reminded him. “I’m going to hit the bathroom and check it out. I’m guessing Whitlow has this entire house bugged, paranoid as he is, but even he wouldn’t snoop in the bathrooms. I hope.”

Max grinned at her. “Don’t be so sure. But I’d guess it’s pretty safe in there. You don’t want to take it out here where someone can walk out of the house any minute.”

“Like now,” she said in a low voice, nodding at Gavin Emery and his wife, Rachel.

“I didn’t get a chance to tell you,” Rachel said as the couple walked toward them, “how very nice it is to meet Bernardo’s brother and sister-in-law.”

“We’re honored that he chose us to take his and Jeanne’s place at the table.”

Gavin looked at Max. “Jed told us you and Bernardo have owned Ferren Arms for nearly thirty years.”

Max nodded. “It was a small handgun company when we bought it, but we had big plans.”

“Lucky for us they worked out. So you’re guaranteeing to deliver the full amount of arms and munitions we need?”

Max dipped his head. “I am. I want to work out the logistics before this meeting breaks up so I can begin to outline what goes where.”

“Listen, I’m going to freshen up before lunch,” Regan broke in and looked at the Emerys. “We’re looking forward to working with all of you.”

And taking you down, she said to herself as she hurried into the house.

Chapter Nine

Luis Rojas had debated with himself for a long time about the wisdom of what he was about to do. He didn't like change in the middle of complex plans, although he'd dealt with it before. Still, this was so complex and of such enormous magnitude that any change could throw an unwanted kink into things. And that would be disastrous.

He'd thought about it and thought about it, quizzed Lorena who had become very irritated with him, but still he couldn't settle it in his mind. Bernardo Ferren was *the* key player in this. He was providing all the arms and munitions for a five-point attack. It wasn't as if they could just highjack a shipload of weapons to fulfill their needs. That worked fine for a local event. No, for something on a national scale— soon to be international— they needed a massive supply, and the Ferrens were providing just that.

When he couldn't put his mind to rest or accept the explanation they'd been given, he decided to check it out himself. He told no one. Lorena would have pitched an unholy fit, and her "partners" would have insisted on getting involved. He didn't need a committee to do this. And if they became that worried, they should have thought of this and acted on it before.

He also could have sent someone to do this for him and saved himself the hassle of the trip. It was something he'd have done under normal circumstances, and he certainly had plenty of other things to attend to. But nothing about this entire project was normal. The scope of it and the vast reach of the results required his personal attention.

The tantalizing image of taking the cartel international filled him with an excitement he hadn't known since the day he became *el jefe*. Under those circumstances he wasn't sure he trusted anyone's observations except his own. Besides, he was the only one who had met Bernardo Ferren in person. If this was a scam of some kind, he'd be able to tell if there was an imposter hanging out in the hospital's cardiac care unit. And if, as Jed Whitlow seemed to believe, the man had actually had a serious heart attack.

So he rearranged his schedule and flew to Denver on his personal jet, landing at the very private airstrip at the home of Hector Infante, one of his major distributors. He always bypassed public airports at all costs for a variety of reasons. Today it was even more important that he not be identified in a public place.

He had dressed for it in jeans and a Denver Broncos T-shirt and cap. He wanted something that didn't smack of "cartel leader" and that would leave people with the memory of a Broncos fan and nothing else. They'd focus so much on his gear they wouldn't even study his face. He had perfected a North American accent to use when he needed it, and he wanted people to remember the outfit, not the man. His research had revealed that Bernardo Ferren was a major supporter of the Broncos, and he was going to turn that to his advantage.

When he jogged down the airstairs and stepped onto the ground, Hector was standing there to greet him, hand extended.

"I am pleased to see you, *jefe*," Hector greeted him, "But to what do I owe this honor? You gave me no hint. Business is good and we have no problems. *Si?*"

Luis nodded. "Business is excellent. It always is in your distribution area."

"Well, then. You also mentioned on the phone you wanted to borrow a truck?" It was obvious he was doing his best to soft-pedal his curiosity.

"I need to do a little snooping," Rojas told him. "Do you perhaps have an inconsequential vehicle I can borrow?"

"Inconsequential?" Hector chuckled. "Is that code for anonymous? Not likely to be tagged by the *policia*? One that blends in?"

"It is." They began to walk away from the plane, trailed by two of Luis's men and one of Hector's. "So, do you have one?"

"Of course." He lowered his voice. "Doesn't every good drug dealer? It's in my parking area." He waved at Luis's attire. "But you won't be very anonymous in that outfit, *mi jefe*."

"That's the idea. They'll remember the shirt and cap and not the man."

"Ah. Of course. Well, here we are."

They had reached the wide graveled space next to the house. Sure enough, among the handful of vehicles sitting there was a gray, four-door pickup, covered in dust and showing its age.

"I only need it for a few hours," Luis told the man.

"It's yours. The keys are in the ignition."

"Thank you, *amigo*." He grinned. "I'll take great care with it."

The two men shook hands. Then Luis climbed into the passenger seat while one of his men took the wheel and the other sat in the back. There was no need for talking. Luis had googled the location of the hospital where Bernardo Ferren was a patient, so there was no need for conversation.

Thirty minutes later, they pulled up to their destination. As soon as the truck stopped, Luis turned to his driver.

"Thirty minutes. No more. That's all I can afford to spend here."

"Si, jefe."

Luis opened the door and climbed out of the truck, entering the hospital's main entrance through an electronic door. He headed at once to a large directory on the wall by the bank of elevators. The cardiac care unit was listed on the third floor. Good. Now to see if he could get access. An elevator opened while he was standing there, disgorging its passengers. He stepped in, pressed three, and waited while other passengers entered. Finally, the doors closed, and the car moved up. He was grateful it only made one stop before hitting three.

The cardiac floor was a bustling place. Halfway down the corridor was a nurses' station, and stretching on either side of it and along the wall across from it were private units with sliding glass doors fronting them, most of which were open at the moment. Nurses and other personnel were moving about, distributing medication, checking patients' conditions. He spotted doctors in a few of the rooms, others had one or two visitors in them. And, in a small conversation area at the far end, a small group of people sat waiting their turn to visit, or speak to a doctor.

What drew his attention the most was one room almost at the end of the corridor. He couldn't see into it at this distance, but a man sat in a chair directly outside the open door. Dressed in slacks and a sweater, there was nothing really remarkable about him except for his posture that reeked of the military.

Interesting. He would have to ask Lorena to find out where Bernardo hired his security guards. Many agencies employed former military, so it wasn't all that unreasonable to think that was the situation here. Still, he wanted to satisfy himself as much as possible.

At the nurses' station in the center of the corridor, two nurses were occupied with paperwork, but what stood out to Rojas was the man in scrubs sitting with him. He could have been cut from the same mold as the other two men. Rojas was sure they were Bernardo's security guards. But there was something about them that put his senses on alert.

He walked slowly down past the row of rooms, staying out of everyone's way, smiling politely in the way of someone with a purpose. He peered quickly into each room as he kept walking until he reached the room next to where the guard sat.

The moment he got close to the room, the man sitting in the chair pinned him with a stare that said *Move and I'll take you apart*. Yes, definitely former military, he decided. He didn't see a weapon, but he knew for damn sure the man had one handy on his person.

What the hell?

The man sitting in the chair rose, all six foot plus of him, and planted himself in front of Luis.

"Can I help you with something?"

"Yes. I, uh, have a friend who works for the Broncos who's here in the ICU. I was told he could have a visitor. He doesn't have much family, so I came here to see him. The problem is, I can't find him."

"That's because you're in the wrong place. And on the wrong floor. This is the coronary care unit. You got off on the wrong floor. Let me help you."

Another man who matched the first two came around the corner just then. Three guards? And this one slid seamlessly into Bernardo's room, opening the door just enough to admit him but not allow anyone to see inside.

Fuck!

Was Bernardo even in there? Was he being held somewhere else while the brother and sister-in-law took his place? Maybe that wasn't even his brother and sister-in-law at the Whitlow lodge. But if they weren't, whoever it was were damn good ringers, according to Lorena.

Something here was off. He had been running the cartel for so long every one of his senses was finely tuned to anything the least little bit off.

"Problem?" he asked.

"This gentleman is looking for his friend, but he's on the wrong floor. I'm just going to get the correct information from the nurses and help him to the elevator."

"Oh, I can find it myself," Luis protested, and dug deep to find a smile. He really wanted to pull out a knife and show this hulk that he could still dismember a man without breaking a sweat. But that wouldn't help his cause, and it would disrupt the image he'd dressed to portray.

"No problem," the bodyguard told him. "It's my pleasure."

I'll bet it is, Luis thought.

"So, who's the big shot in the room you guys are guarding?" he asked as nonchalantly as he could while he was being smoothly hustled down toward the elevator.

"Big shot?"

"Yeah. He must have some juice to have two of you guys watching him."

"Oh. No big shot. That's our uncle. We're with him because he doesn't have any other family."

Yeah, right.

"That's very nice of you guys."

"That's us, just a couple of nice guys. And here's your elevator. I hope your friend is okay."

Luis had to admit the guy was smooth. He himself was no novice at this stuff, but before he could even say thank you, he was in the elevator and on the way to the fourth floor. He'd be riding a few extra minutes but it didn't matter. He'd gotten what he came for. At least part of it. He pushed the button for the lobby but had to wait for the elevator car to make two stops going up before it headed down again.

The pickup truck pulled up to the entrance just as he exited the building. He climbed in, motioned for them to get moving, and pulled a burner phone from his pocket. He had the home phone numbers for both Ferren brothers. He pinched in the one for Bernardo. A female answered.

"Ferren residence."

Luis had done his homework. Bernardo and Jeanne Ferren had a housekeeper, so he was sure she was the one answering the phone.

"Yes. May I please speak to Jeanne Ferren?"

"I'm so sorry but she's unavailable right now." The voice was deliberately anonymous.

"Well, can you tell me when I might speak with her? I'm sure she'll want to take my call."

"Oh, I'm so sorry. Her husband has had a massive heart attack, and she is spending every spare moment in the hospital with him."

Well, that was a big fat fucking lie.

"I'm sorry to hear that. What hospital? Perhaps I can stop by and pay my respects."

"I'm sorry," the voice said again, "but he's not allowed visitors. If you could leave me your name and phone number, I can pass this along to Mrs. Ferren."

"That's all right. I'll just try her next time I'm in town again." He clicked off the call.

All his antennae were vibrating, and he was damn sure those men at the hospital weren't private guards hired by the Ferrens. But who, then? He'd say they were government agents except he was positive there was no way in hell word of what was going on had leaked. The people involved had too much to lose. Besides, their avid hunger for power would make them doubly cautious. But something was definitely up here.

Next, he tried Max Ferren's number, and a man answered. Luis tried to remember everything he'd learned about Max and his wife since Lorena had told him about the switch. Did they have a live-in male? This guy didn't sound like any servant he'd ever heard. A bodyguard? If so, what was he doing at their house instead of guarding them at the meeting.

"I'm sorry," the man said, "but Mr. and Mrs. Ferren are away for a few days. If you give me your name and phone number, I can pass a message along to them when they get back."

"That's okay. I just thought I'd try and hook up with them while I was in town. I'll try them again next time."

He disconnected and sat there holding the phone, thinking. They could drive by both Ferren houses and see who was actually there, but he didn't want to give anyone a chance to get a good look at him.

"Back to the plane," he told his driver. He had to

think about this.

After returning the truck, he thanked Hector for his assistance.

"I'll be calling you again shortly," he told the man, "about the action we discussed."

He had brought each of his top-level distributors into this along with key lieutenants and prepped them for what was coming. He was being tasked with providing the manpower and they would need a great deal of it.

"As we've discussed," he told the man, "this has to be carefully executed. America has a lot of military power, and we have to cut off their legs and take control before they have a chance to react."

"It is an honor, *jefe*," Hector told him. "I await your call."

It wasn't until they were back on the plane and in the air, and he was seated with a drink in his hand, that he made the next call. As expected, it went to voice mail, so he left a message. Fifteen minutes passed, and he was on his second drink when his cell rang.

"What is it?" Lorena hissed. "You know we are all meeting. We're finally down to the rest of the details. I'll let you know when I have the information you need." She paused. "You and your men are still ready, yes? You're not calling to tell me you've changed your mind, I hope."

"Why would I change my mind? When this happens, the world will be my marketplace, with international distribution."

"Then what is so important?" she demanded.

He took a sip of his drink. "I hope I'm wrong, but I think we've been made."

"What?" She squeaked the word, although she still kept her voice low enough. "Damn it. That's impossible. What makes you think that?"

"I decided to check out the situation with the Ferren brothers myself. I went—"

"You did what?" Her voice had dropped twenty decibels and two octaves, a very bad sign. "Without checking with me first? Discussing it?"

"Fuck it, Lorena. Even though I don't have a so-called seat at the table, I'm as much a part of this as you and the others. Agreed?"

"Yes, yes, yes. Tell me what you did? Luis, if you've blown this—"

"Give me some credit, will you?" Sometimes he just wanted to smack her.

There was a short pause. "All right. Tell me exactly

want you did and what you discovered."

He explained about the trip to Denver and getting to the hospital when she interrupted him again.

"I can't believe you were stupid enough to just walk into that hospital. What if someone saw you?"

"They did, as a matter of fact, which was exactly what I wanted."

He told her about his outfit and why he chose it, and about the guards at Bernardo's room in the CCU.

"They could easily have come from a high-end security company," he said, "but just as easily be government guns."

"In which case your outfit wouldn't do you a bit of good. They're trained to see past that and memorize faces, whether they are current or former military. Damn, Luis." Another pause. "Okay, tell me every single one of the details. I'm going to have to let the others know about this."

When he finished, he was met with complete silence, silence that stretched so long he wondered if she was even still there.

"Lorena?" he asked at last.

"I'm here. I trust your judgment, Luis. Also, we've known each other a long time. You aren't an alarmist. Extra careful, yes. And with good reason. But an alarmist? That's not you. These people have to be from the government, and not from a department any of us are familiar with."

"Not Homeland Security?"

"Maybe a specialized area. And if Bernardo is truly not at the hospital, the only reason they could have for maintaining the illusion is because they've got him squirreled away someplace until they can bring us down. I can't imagine how they even got into this. We've been beyond careful. But if this is true, then the Max and Regan Ferren at Jed's lodge are ringers. And damn good ones, I might add."

"What do you mean?"

"They look exactly like the pictures we've seen of them."

"Maybe the government had them go through plastic surgery," he suggested.

"That would mean they were onto us long before now, and I don't think that's true, They'd have found a way to act as soon as they stumbled on the information."

"Let me think a moment." Silence hummed across the connection. "We are through for the day, although I'm sure the discussion will continue through dinner. And you aren't the only one who's leery of the new couple. They're almost too good to be true."

"Exactamente!"

"Let me get Elias alone and run this past him before I reach out to the others. As long as these people are here, they can't do us any harm."

"Don't bet on it," Rojas warned her. "Keep an eye on any attempts to make phone calls or communicate in any other way."

"And what way would that be?" she retorted. "They won't be leaving the premises. In fact, I might pull Jed to the side after I speak with Elias and see if there's some way he can have their car disabled."

"Don't do anything to raise red flags," he cautioned. "Besides, you may not want to do that. When they leave, Whitlow can arrange to have someone track them and see where they go and who they see."

"Luis, we are three weeks away from the big day. We have to do this very carefully so it doesn't blow up in our faces." She gave a humorless laugh. "So to speak."

"Call me later and give me an update," he insisted. "And if you need anything from me, all you have to do is ask."

"I'll keep that in mind."

After the call ended, Rojas had the steward bring him another drink and sat back in deep thought. One important fact had to be unearthed. Who in the fucking hell had discovered what they were planning and put a plan in motion? That was a key piece of information. If it was any part of the government, he hoped it wasn't the Department of Homeland Security. Those fuckers were relentless and had incredible resources they could tap into. That would present an even bigger problem.

He sipped his drink, sitting back in his chair, and hoped to hell his whole carefully constructed organization wasn't going to fall apart or be destroyed because his hunger for money and power had made him agree to be a part of this plot.

Chapter Ten

Silas Branson was sitting at his desk, studying a report and wondering how things at the cabal meeting were going when one of the cell phones on his desk rang. It was the line he'd set up dedicated to this mission, now titled Operation: Zeus, for the Greek god of law, order, and justice. Only select people had the number.

He glanced at his watch as he reached for the receiver. Not quite dinnertime yet. Assuming he wouldn't be hearing from Max or Regan until later in the evening, he frowned as he lifted the receiver.

"Branson."

"Sir," a deep masculine voice said, "this is Kaminski at the hospital in Denver. I think we may have a problem."

Immediately, Si's hand tensed on the phone, but he forced himself to remain calm. *Get the details, assess the situation then decide if you need to panic.*

"Give me the details."

"We had an odd situation here just a few minutes ago. A man showed up in the CCU who said he was looking for a friend. He was dressed in Broncos gear, and he told me his friend worked for the team. But he showed a lot of interest in the subject's room here, even though he tried to hide it."

"He didn't get into the room, did he?" Si demanded. He immediately regretted it because he had two of his best men on this job.

"No, he did not. Peralta came around the corner from the head just at that moment. Guy said his friend was in the ICU so I explained he was on the wrong floor. Left Peralta standing guard while I ushered the guy to the elevator. But he was too curious about Bernardo, and I have a feeling he might know the room is empty. Then again, maybe I'm just making too much of this. I know we have to deal in facts, but—"

"No, no," Si broke in. "Intuition has saved more asses than anything."

"Peralta and I discussed it, and we agree whoever this guy was, he scared the shit out of the subject."

"Did he say anything about it?"

"He did ask what the man wanted, and if he'd left. But Ferren—the subject—has been nervous as a virgin on her wedding night ever since. He asked if he could call his wife, and I told him I'd have to check with you."

"Describe the man."

"About five ten," Kaminski told him. "Thick black hair with some gray in it. About middle fifties. I took him for Hispanic, but he didn't have a trace of an accent."

"That means nothing. He could have lived here for a long time or taught himself to speak without it." He drummed his fingers on the desk. "And the guy just left?"

"Yes, sir."

The only Hispanic Si could connect to Operation: Zeus was Luis Rojas, head of the powerful cartel involved in this abomination being planned. But would Rojas himself come to scout out a situation? Maybe, if he didn't think he could trust any of his men to get a proper read on the situation. But what had put a bug up his ass?

He was still thinking about letting Ferren call his wife when a clicking sound broke in. He looked at the screen and saw another call was coming in.

"Kowalski, can you hold for one? I have a call I have to check."

If it was coming in on this cell phone, it was definitely important. "Branson."

"Sir, this is Lane Vardan at the Bernardo Ferren house. Mrs. B's babysitter."

Si chuckled. "And how's that going today?"

"About the same."

"Was there something specific you needed? I've got Kaminski holding on the other line. He had a little situation at the hospital today."

"I wonder if it has anything to do with the phone call."

Every one of Si's nerves went on alert. "What phone call?"

"The one I just answered. A man claiming to be a friend of the Ferrens called asking for Mrs. F. I told him she wasn't home. That her husband had a heart attack. You know the drill. He said he was pretty sure she'd want to take the call. I asked him to leave a number, and he hung up."

Si blew out a breath. "We definitely have a situation here." He told her about the visitor at the hospital. "Did their phone register the number of the incoming?"

"Yes. I'll text it to you but my instincts tell me it's a burner and won't do us any good."

"I'm sure you're right. Okay, text me the number and hang tight with Mrs. Ferren. Tell her no hospital visits today, even if you have to tie her up and sit on her."

Lane chuckled. "No worries. I've got this covered."

"I bet you do. Thanks."

Lane Vardan was one of his best agents. If anyone could handle the volatile Jeanne Ferren, it was her.

He clicked back over to Kaminski and gave him a brief version of Lane's call.

"Someone wants to get in touch with the Ferrens for sure," he said. "I'll check the tap we installed on Max Ferren's phone to see if he got any calls, but I think we've stirred up some interest here before we wanted to. I'll have to figure out how and why. Meanwhile, keep a close eye on Bernardo. Your night relief will be there around eight as usual."

"Okay," Kaminski said. "Peralta and I will brief them in detail, although the incident didn't last that long. But if we caught someone's interest already and they did something this bold, no telling what will happen next."

"True. I've got to find a way to get in touch with the fake Ferrens and put them on alert without warning anyone they're with what I'm doing."

"Well. Good luck with that."

Si snorted. "Thanks."

After he disconnected the call, he sat there for a moment, thinking. He had to warn Max and Regan that their cover might be blown without tipping off the people they were with. Then he had to figure out how to get support into the area so they had backup without anyone knowing about it. And then he had to get them out of there without the people in this nasty little group reacting in a bad way. He hoped to hell both Max and Regan had made good use of their electronic pens because they'd need all the proof they could get on this one.

Okay, first he'd text Max a code phrase they'd decided on. It had to be something that wouldn't raise any eyebrows in case, god forbid, someone was looking over his shoulder when he read the message. He picked up the cell he used only to communicate with Max and typed in, *Order will be ready*. It was code for, *Call me ASAP*. If anyone asked, he could tell them it was from the factory, from the person they'd tapped to handle this while Bernardo was recuperating and he was at this meeting. Hopefully that wouldn't raise any eyebrows.

*****

At that very moment, Max was standing on the patio at the lodge with the rest of the unholy group, trying to do more listening than talking. The afternoon had been devoted to analyzing the timing of each event, whether they should all happen at the same time or one after the other. Where each of the couples should be when it happened. At home, was the prevailing opinion.

Max did his best to find out what the plans were after that. The best he could get was they would have observers at each site and convene the next morning to move forward from there. They touched briefly on the steps they would take to put their own people in place but not nearly as much as Max had hoped they would. He didn't want to push and call undue attention to himself, any more than his arrival already had.

Immediately after the afternoon meeting broke up, he and Regan had begged a few minutes to unpack their suitcases. Jed followed them upstairs to show them which room was theirs and hung around the doorway. He and Regan took their time with the suitcases until Jed finally left them alone.

Regan closed and locked the bedroom door. "He knows something's not right."

"Yeah, but he's got no proof. And Si still has the real Max and Regan locked down so tight that no one will ever find them without him."

"Someone definitely went through my stuff," Max told her.

"Mine, too. But they did it so well if we hadn't left markers, we'd never have known it."

"Still, we need to be prepared for anything."

Max opened the concealed compartment in his suitcase and took out two handguns and a holster. Regan took the thigh holster and fastened it in place then fit the smaller of the handguns into it. Max shoved his into the small of his back where his bulky sweater covered it. He also took out the extra cell phones Si had given him and turned them on. He handed one to Regan. "Just in case."

They both hid them in a pouch under the bathroom sink. Not a place anyone was likely to look for something.

He finally had a chance to tell Regan about his call earlier to Si, which had been short and sharp. Si was more sickened than shocked at the targets that had been selected. He told Max to hang tight and he'd get back to him. He needed to consult with his boss and make some preparations.

"But check in with me every few hours," he said.

Now he and Regan were outside, mingling and being pleasant yet remote with the others. This wasn't a touchy-feely group for sure. And he was getting the third degree with a thin veneer of courtesy. But Max had years of training in evading questions, of giving answers that weren't really answers. He could tell they were getting frustrated.

At the moment he was holding a drink in one hand, standing with Emery and Cavanaugh, hoping to pick up some more nuggets of information. He had his phone on silent, so if he hadn't had his hand in his pocket, he might never have felt the vibration. No one had the number except Si, so it had to be damn important for him to call right now since they'd spoken just recently.

He drained his glass and set it down.

"Think I need a pit stop before I have another one," he told the two men. "Back in a second."

In the downstairs bathroom, he locked the door and pulled out his phone, every muscle in his body tightening at the text on the screen.

Order is ready.

That was their code for shit is hitting the fan. Damn it all to hell.

He punched in the secure number he'd been given.

Si answered at once. "We may have a problem."

Just what he didn't need. "What happened?"

He listened while Si gave him an abbreviated version of the incident at the hospital plus the information on the two other phone calls. "I'm so close to getting the rest of the information we need." He checked his watch. "Listen, I can only stay in here another minute or someone will get suspicious. "Give me at least tonight and tomorrow morning. Then I'll figure out how to get us out of here."

"Be damn careful. As soon as I got the call, I had George and Kevin loaded up in a helicopter. I got hold of Lou Valenti. He gave me a location for them to land, and he'll have a car waiting for them. He'll help them get close enough for extraction if you need it. I have three additional men going with them, and they have every weapon and gadget they'll need if push comes to shove. The chopper will also stay there to get you the hell out of there if you need it."

"Damn, Si. I hope it doesn't come to that."

"Are you and Regan both armed?"

"Yes." He was also damned glad that along with the other goodies, Si had given each of them a watch that had a GPS locator in it. He hoped he wouldn't need to use it, but just in case, Si would be able to locate either of them.

"Okay. Stay alert and stay alive."

"That's the plan."

He had just pocketed the phone again when there was a knock on the bathroom door.

"Is anyone in here?"

"I'll be right out," he called.

He yanked the door open to find Elizabeth Emery standing there.

"Oh! I'm so sorry. I didn't want to have to run upstairs."

"No problem. It's all yours."

When he walked out onto the patio again, he saw Regan standing with Gavin Emery, Elizabeth's husband, and Hildie Cavanagh. He wondered if they were all just being sociable or if each member of the group was tasked with getting their own read on Max and Regan. What better place to do it than in the so-called relaxing atmosphere after the tense all-day meeting. He'd have to find a way to pass along Si's information without rousing anyone's suspicions.

He eased up beside her and casually slid an arm around her waist.

"I was just telling Gavin how beautiful it is here and how glad we are to have this opportunity to see it. Maybe we could look at buying some property around here."

"I understand Colorado is just as beautiful," Hildie commented, looking at Regan over the rim of her glass.

"It is." Regan nodded. "But it's nice to have some other place to spend time on a regular basis. You know, away from everyone else."

Hildie smiled, what Regan would call an artificial curve of the lips. "You should come visit us when you can. We had one meeting at our ranch, and Bernardo and Jeanne loved it."

Max was thankful for Si's very detailed briefing. "I thought you met twice there? At least that's what my brother told me, and I remember the trips."

"Oh. Right." Her laugh dripped with ice. "How stupid of me not to remember that, but it was one of our earliest meetings."

"Of course."

And that's a big fat lie, Max thought. We're not even close to being out of the woods yet.

"Okay, everyone." Anna Whitlow clapped her hands. "The steaks are ready, and everything else is set up on the buffet table. Please help yourselves."

They ate at the umbrella tables on the patio. Max and Regan ended up with the Alvaros, not his favorite couple. In fact, although it wasn't blatantly obvious, they had maneuvered the seating to end up this way. By the time the meal was over, Max felt as if they'd been given the third degree by someone as expert at it as anyone he'd ever met.

It was after eight by the time the patio was cleared. He was pretty sure Anna Whitlow didn't do any of her clearing and washing up except at these meetings. Nor, he thought, did the other women, but you had to make adjustments when you were plotting to overthrow your government. Of course, considering the subject matter, he wouldn't have wanted anyone around, either. He wondered where the hell Whitlow's security guards were hiding and what they thought about all this? Of course, the kind of men he hired and the money he paid them, they probably didn't give a rip as long as they got their paychecks.

Si's info had mentioned that all the others also had a security staff, but he didn't know if they were around. All extraneous bodies were conspicuously absent.

At the top of Max's list was finding a way to talk to Regan and call Si without hiding in one of the bathrooms. He wandered over to Jed Whitlow, who had just walked into the great room. "This place you've got here is terrific. A beautiful piece of land."

"Thanks. We bought it years ago and love coming up here whenever we can."

Max nodded. "It's certainly a great place for these meetings. Away from the world. Out of sight of everyone else."

"Yes, it's worked out well. Listen, how about a drink? We usually try to chill out at the end of the day."

"That sounds great, but Regan and I thought we might stretch our legs a little after sitting all day. Is it safe to walk around out here at night? Any wild animals roaming around?"

Whitlow studied him for a moment, as if trying to read any meaning behind his words.

"They mostly don't bother us unless we bother them. I used to use this place for hunting, but I've kind of lost my taste for it in recent years. More important things to focus on." He winked. "If you stick close to the lodge, you'll be fine. Beyond that, there's not many places you can walk anyway."

"We won't be long." He looked around the room. "Anyone want to join us?"

Thank god they all turned him down.

"No? Okay. We'll be back shortly to join you for drinks."

The moment they were outside he took Regan's hand and fast-walked her to the edge of the trees and just into the thicket.

"Okay," she said when they stopped. "What's put a bug in your ear? I don't believe you just wanted a whiff of the night air."

"I had to find a way to talk to you without hiding in the bathroom. Si called. We have a problem."

"How bad?"

"We don't know, but it could blow up in our faces, if you'll pardon the pun."

Then he laid it all out for her. He was pleased to note that her reaction was calm and levelheaded, even though he was sure she was as much on edge as he was.

"Do they know for sure it was Rojas at the hospital?"

"Yes. Kaminski, one of the agents guarding the room, took his picture with the camera in his watch. Then Si ran it through their facial recognition software." He shook his head. "That's probably the phone call Lorena Alvaro excused herself to take."

Regan frowned. "Wonder why she hasn't figured out how to pass that info along to the others."

"Waiting for the right time, is my guess. After all,

we're here where they have eyes on us at all times. She may be telling them as we speak."

Regan shuddered. "There's a pleasant thought."

"Listen." Max cupped her chin and tilted her face up to him. "I'm sure this is a lot more than you bargained for. I can arrange a way with Si to have you extracted."

She shook her head. "Not unless you leave, too. I knew what I was signing on for, Max. It's bastards like these who got Dylan killed. I'm not leaving until we have the goods to take them down."

"You know I'll protect you with my life."

"I do." She put her arms around him and curled herself against his body, her warmth seeping into him. "But I hope it doesn't come to that." She paused. "Max? You think they'll let us leave?"

"I think if this looks like it's going to blow up, they might try to stop us, which is why I'm going to make some calls while we're out here. Si said to contact Lou Valenti, the sheriff. Also, Bone Frog is sending Kevin and George out here in a chopper along with some additional firepower in case we need it." He waited, wondering how she would react to this sudden escalation of danger.

"Well, we knew it probably wouldn't be a

cakewalk. Make your calls, and let's set up some contingencies. Hopefully we'll still be able to drive out of here, meet the chopper, and get the hell away."

"Agreed."

"Okay," she told him. "We need to keep in mind that the most important thing is to get as much additional information as we can. Somehow, we need to find out who the puppet is they plan to install when the government falls."

"That ought to be on the agenda pretty quickly, don't you think?"

Regan nodded. "I listen to all this and I keep seeing visions of Third World countries."

"Because that's exactly what it is," Max agreed. "No doubt about it. Okay, I think we're far enough from the house so I can make my calls."

He pulled out his encrypted cell phone and hit the number for the sheriff. Whatever happened, even if he didn't make it, he was going to make damn sure Regan did.

Chapter Eleven

Lorena Alvaro filled her wineglass and glanced at her husband, who nodded. Then she cleared her throat.

"Excuse me, everyone. We need to take advantage of the fact that the Ferrens are out of the room for the moment and discuss something that's come up. Something very important and worrisome."

Jed looked over at her.

"Is it about Max and Regan Ferren? I wonder if I'm the only one here who thinks there's something not right there. I can't put my finger on it, even though I spent two days with them."

"They're almost too good to be true." Gavin Emery's gravelly voice rattled in the air. "I said that from the beginning."

"Exactly," Lorena agreed. "And they might very well be. You won't be happy with what I have to say. Things aren't exactly as we've been led to believe."

"Well, what the hell is it?" Kurt Cavanaugh demanded. "Don't keep us waiting. We have enough to be on edge about."

"All right." She let out a breath. "I know Luis can be a bit uncontainable at times but he can usually sniff out trouble."

She went on to give them the details of her phone call from him, being sure to include every bit of information. When she finished, everyone stared at her for a moment.

Then Gavin smacked his fist on the arm of his chair. "Damn it, Lorena, I know that bastard Rojas has put a lot of money in our pockets and is providing the manpower we need. But hell. This is a very delicate operation. Any little thing could upset it. He can't go off like that without checking with us first."

Lorena's smile held little humor. "I'm not sure I want to be the one to tell him that. When I brought you all into my arrangement with him, giving him a wider choice of travel routes, none of you objected to the millions rolling your way from his drug sales. I believe I'm correct in that?" She looked around.

"That doesn't give him the right to go off on his own like that," Jed reminded her. "This all has to be closely coordinated or it can easily fall apart. What if he tickled someone's curiosity? One slip of someone's tongue, one wrong move—"

She held up her hand. "We all know that. Luis

does, too. But if we have a ringer here with us, it can affect him as much as it does us."

"So, are you saying this isn't the real Max and Regan Ferren?" Anna Whitlow asked.

"I'm saying we don't know for sure," Lorena answered, "but it looks suspicious. *He's* very suspicious after the hospital visit. He's convinced something doesn't add up, such as perhaps Bernardo isn't even in that hospital room. Didn't even have a heart attack or open-heart surgery. He said they all but threw him into the elevator. He certainly didn't get a look at Bernardo."

"So he couldn't see if Bernardo was even in the room?" Hildie asked.

Lorena shook her head. "Luis never got a chance to find out. He said the men were very smooth in the way they got him out of the area."

Gavin took a swallow of his drink. "And what's so secretive about a man recuperating from open-heart surgery anyway? Why does he need men like that guarding him?"

"It may be the same men who were there when I went to see him," Jed pointed out. "Their company does a lot of under-the-table business, especially in foreign countries. The group on the losing side isn't always so happy with him. And he's very vulnerable in the hospital. Anyone could get to him in his condition. It sounded reasonable at the time."

"Here's what I want to know." Kurt rose and began to pace the great room. "Why is it necessary to have so many guards there who, according to Luis, look like they came from a Special Ops unit? Why are the drapes closed over the window and the door to his room, unless it's to hide the fact the room is empty? Why was there a guy who couldn't look more out of place be sitting at the nurses' station? And where the hell is Jeanne Ferren?"

"Jed, I know this man is a friend of yours. That's why we accepted him, but—"

Jed glared at everyone. "You all accepted him because he could supply the weapons and munitions we needed for this. It wasn't as if we could put this job out for bid."

"But are you sure we should be doing business with someone who deals with the kind of people who necessitate that kind of protection?" Elizabeth Emery asked.

"Exactly what kind of people do you imagine us contacting for something like this?" Jed barked a laugh. "And Bernardo was a known quantity who has the same goals we do. Don't get a holier-than-thou attitude, Elizabeth. We're not much better. Think of the people who will be killed when we launch our program." He looked around the room. "Anyone want to change their minds?" He waited for the space of two heartbeats. "No? Okay, then let's move along."

"Here's a question." Gavin cleared his throat. "If this couple here are ringers, where are the real Max and Regan Ferren?"

Jed stopped pacing. "A good question."

Elias, who hadn't said much, went to the bar to refill his glass then turned to everyone. "Lorena has passed along what little Rojas learned. That's all we have at the moment. We can't exactly start asking questions to see what's really going on. Does anyone have any suggestions about where to proceed from here? Do we think Jed should go to Denver again and see what's going on?"

"And call attention to us and our project?" Elizabeth Emery wet her lips. "Surely people as smart as we are can figure out what in the hell is going on here and what to do about it." She looked around. "And, in case it's slipped anyone's mind, we need to make damn sure the shipments we ordered are still a go and will be delivered on time."

“Max—either real or fake—assured us they are,” Lorena said. “Let’s pin him on it in the morning.”

“Assuming the worst,” Lorena broke in, “and these are imposters, does anyone have any idea how someone got word of our plans and set us up?”

“Fuck no, and that’s disturbing.” Kurt raked his fingers through his hair. “We’re hardly stupid people. We should have some ideas here. Tomorrow we’re going to discuss the exact steps after the incidents on the Fourth as well as how we’re handling the person we’re putting in the top slot, and if these people—”

“That person has to remember he’s just a figurehead,” Hildie interrupted. “That’s it.”

“Not a problem. All he wants is the publicity and the glory. The moment we take control of Congress and remove the president, we’ll be in control. All the way.”

Anna cleared her throat. “I hate to ask at this late date—and I am not doubting anyone, especially my husband—but are you sure this is going to work? We have so much invested in it.”

“Like a charm,” Lorena answered. “We’ve all worked and planned very hard for it. You know that better than anyone. Put enough money in the right hands so when disaster strikes, we have people begging us to take over. The world will most definitely be our oyster."

"Then we'd better figure out whether the two people who are right now probably returning from their stroll in the moonlight are the real deal or not."

"Maybe we shouldn't have let them outside by themselves." This came from Kurt.

"Just how would you have us stop them?" Jed asked. "Tell them they can't go anywhere by themselves?"

"It doesn't matter," Kurt interjected. "They can't go anywhere without us knowing, and it gave us a chance to learn this information. But, somehow, we have to validate them. Make sure they are the real Regan and Max Ferren."

"Exactly how are we going to do that?" Hildie Kavanaugh demanded. "It's not as if we can take their fingerprints and run them through a database."

"If Bernardo's in the hospital—or even if he's somewhere else—and Max is here, who's running the factory?" Gavin asked.

"Their general manager," Jed answered. "I called him when I was in Denver and again before I met with the real-or-not-real Max and Regan. Told him I was just checking on things. Bernardo had involved him from the start. He said sometimes both of the brothers are away at the same time. He's been with the company for fifteen years, so he can handle it during those times."

"Well." Lorena looked around the room. "Does anyone have any suggestions that are practical and make sense? I'd say after Luis's trip this whole thing is very suspicious. And why are they out there taking a walk by themselves anyway? This isn't exactly a place where you stroll around at night, Jed. Are they hiding something? We cannot afford anything to go wrong. Not at this point."

No one said a word.

"Have you picked up anything on the bugs in their room?" Kurt wanted to know.

Jed shook his head. "Not a thing. In fact, it's almost as if they know I've got listening devices in there and they're performing for them. Same thing at the hotel."

"They can't be too worried about them," Kurt pointed out, "or they'd have brought jammers with them. Not that people like having their privacy invaded, but they're behaving exactly like people who have nothing to hide."

"And maybe they don't." Then she paused,

forehead wrinkled in thought. "This all happened so fast, and we only have Rojas's word for it that something's off. There is, however, something else that concerns me. Jed, when you went to visit Bernardo, you saw Jeanne, right?"

He nodded. "And I gave her the number of your cell phone, as you requested. I also gave her Anna's, just in case."

"Right." Anna nodded. "Because we know none of their regular friends know about this group, and I thought she might need someone here to talk to. Maybe get some moral support while her husband recovers from open-heart surgery. Anyway, she has not called once. Wouldn't one of us have heard from her if there was a problem?"

"Assuming she still has the cell phone and is able to call."

Silence blanketed the room while they digested what the Whitlows had said.

"Well." Lorena cleared her throat. "We need a way to confirm if these people are the real Ferrens or not. And if they aren't, who sent them? Tomorrow we're going to be discussing what happens after July 4th and how we proceed. If we have a ringer here, we have to take care of that first."

Gavin nodded. “Agreed. We need to do some serious thinking and come up with possible solutions. For right now, however, I suggest that we break up this little pow-wow. If the Ferrens walk back into the house and see us congregated here, they’re liable to get suspicious.”

“Right,” Jed added. “We don’t want them to get the idea we’re having a meeting without them. We’d just raise their suspicions if we’re wrong in our assumptions.”

“I agree,” Gavin Emery said. “Elias, I have some brand-new imported cigars if you’d like to join me on the patio and indulge.”

“Go ahead,” Lorena urged her husband. “After all this, I have the start of a headache. I think I’ll take something for it and turn in early.”

“Me, too,” Elizabeth Emery echoed.

“I have some calls to make.” Kurt Cavanaugh rose from the easy chair where he’d been sitting. “I guess I’ll head upstairs, too.”

“Anna, why don’t you fix some tea for yourself before you go upstairs,” Jed suggested. “I’ll be along after a while. I have some work to do down here before I call it a day.”

“That’s a good idea. Let me just clean up the

glasses here."

Jed was still sitting in the great room with his laptop, searching for anything he could find on the Ferrens, when the front door opened and the Ferrens walked back in. He closed the laptop and stood.

"Oh, don't bother to get up," Regan said.

"Right," Max agreed. "If you've work to do, don't let us interrupt."

"It's nothing that can't wait. How was the walk?" He managed a grin. "No wild animals, right?"

"Right." Max looked around the room. "Everyone gone to bed?"

"Most of them. Gavin and Elias are out on the patio smoking cigars. I'm sure they'd love to have you join them."

Max grinned. "Thanks. But I think my wife would shoot me if I indulged."

"We should turn in early, too," Regan urged. "It's been a long day, and I'm sure tomorrow will be even longer. We'll be discussing the next steps, right? At least that's how Bernardo told us it would go."

Jed managed to keep the pleasant expression on his face. "That's the plan."

"Then we'll see you in the morning."

"Sure I can't offer you a drink?" He'd play the

gracious host if it killed him. Besides, what better way to avoid raising their suspicions, just in case they weren't the real deal.

"No, but thanks anyway."

"Okay, then. Breakfast at nine and then we get to work. See you then."

He watched them climb the stairs, trying to read their body language and determine if they were even truly married. He saw nothing that raised any red flags. If they were ringers, they were damn good at doing this. And that sent a heavy chill down his spine.

*****

Max closed the door to their room, wishing the doors had locks. The vibes he got from Jed when they returned to the house made all his senses send out warnings. What the hell had happened while they were outside?

"I think I'll take a shower before turning in."

Although his tone was casual, his body was tense. Every one of his senses was on high alert. Something was going on here. He had no idea what, but he'd bet it had to do with that scum Luis Rojas checking out Bernardo Ferren's hospital situation. He'd learned in the SEALs that you could plan every mission down to the last detail, but you couldn't do much for the unexpected.

Regan glanced at him and nodded her understanding. "I think I will, too. You go first."

He stripped off his clothes, tossed them on a chair, and walked naked into the bathroom. Once he had the spray adjusted the way he wanted, he stepped into it and took one of the quickest showers ever. Regan took his place and did the same thing. Then they wrapped in towels and left the water running while they took advantage of the opportunity to talk.

"Something's weird here," she said. "I could feel it when we stepped back into the house."

Max nodded. "Yeah, me, too. You know Rojas called Lorena and gave her every little detail plus his assessment."

"And *you* know they discussed it while we were outside. I just wish we had some way to know what happens next."

Regan blotted water from her hair with one corner of the towel. "Do you think they'll actually get into a discussion tomorrow of what comes next? I mean, if they think we're not the real thing?"

He shrugged. "Hard to say. I'm sure Jed has done everything he can to make sure this goes forward. It's unfortunate that Luis Rojas decided to take matters into his own hands and visit Bernardo. However, Si is on top of it, and reinforcements are arriving tonight and rendezvousing with Lou Valenti. If we have to fight our way out of here tomorrow, at least we won't be on our own."

"Are you going to connect with Si tomorrow?"

Max nodded. In the morning before breakfast. Then I have to signal him on the secure cell once every hour. It's set up so I can tap one button and it sends the right signal to him. If there's trouble, I tap a different button."

"And if all hell breaks loose?"

"Then I call him and tell him to have everyone get their asses here ASAP." He pulled her against him, his arm around her body. God. She felt so good. "And when this is over..." His voice trailed off.

Regan nodded. "When this is over."

"Meanwhile, I think I need a good-night kiss or I won't sleep."

She laughed. "Okay, sailor, pucker up."

He was glad that in the grip of danger, personal as well as national, she still had a sense of humor. When this was all over, he definitely was not letting her go.

Chapter Twelve

Jed Whitlow was shaving the next morning, standing at the bathroom sink wearing just a towel wrapped around his waist, when his wife walked in, holding her cell phone.

"I have a question."

He rinsed his razor and stroked it through another line of cream. "Okay. Shoot."

"Do you think I should try and call Jeanne? Maybe she isn't sure if she should contact us. Or it might be that Bernardo is worried that somehow whoever has them squirreled away has set up a way to trace cell calls."

Jed thought for a moment while he shaved the rest of his face. Finished, he rinsed the razor, knocked it against the sink for good measure, and wiped his face.

"Good point," he acknowledged at last. "It might be worth the chance, though, to see if we have enemies in our midst."

"Okay. I'm going to call her right now before we go downstairs."

Jed watched as she brought up her contacts list,

found the number for Jeanne Ferren, and hit Dial. He waited, watching, but nothing happened.

"Don't leave a message," he ordered. "If they hit redial, all they'll get is the burner phone you're using."

"You're right." She disconnected and put the cell in the pocket of her slacks. "I'll try her again later. I'll just go on downstairs, put the breakfast casseroles in to heat, warm up the pastries, and make sure the coffeemaker is on."

"I'll be down in just a couple of minutes. Keep an eye on the Ferrens and see if you spot anything wrong."

She sighed, "I will, but I'm not sure I'd even know if something was off."

"Use your intuition. You've got great instincts."

Anna flashed him a quick smile. "If you say so. I'm not so sure they're working if I didn't spot anything wrong with the Ferrens, even after we spent two days with them."

Jed snorted. "Don't sell yourself short. I didn't, either. Remember?"

She frowned. "And don't you think that's weird? You, especially, are a great judge of people."

"I think I was prepared not to like them because I was pissed off about Bernardo's heart attack, callous bastard that I am."

She shook her head. "We've been planning this for so long that the possibility of something unexpected screwing it all up was the overriding factor. They might not be our cup of tea but then not everyone in this group is. We became united by a common enemy and then decided to attack that enemy and change things."

"You're right." He hung his towel on a hook and walked naked into the bedroom, still talking as he dressed. "I'm getting a real bad feeling about things though. And about what we might have to do to fix this."

She walked over to stand in front of him, placing her hand gently on his cheek. "But you'll handle it. You always do."

"Thanks for your confidence." He gave her a quick kiss on the lips. "Okay, go ahead and get breakfast ready. We'll need the energy."

*****

Max and Regan were also awake. They'd been up since early that morning, hiding in the bathroom so they could talk softly without fear of being overheard.

"I have this bad feeling that won't go away," Regan told him. "I call it my doomsday sense. Usually it means something very bad is going to happen."

Max pulled her into his arms and kissed her forehead. God, he loved the feel of her against him. No matter what happened, he was going to make sure she didn't get hurt.

"I should tell you you're imagining things, but I have the same little quirk. It saved my ass a lot of times in the SEALs. Even the day I got shot, it could have been so much worse if I hadn't had that little voice whispering in my ear."

"I'm glad it wasn't worse," she murmured against his shoulder.

He gave a short laugh. "Yeah, me, too."

"What are we going to do, Max? I just know something bad is going to happen today."

"I'm going to call Si right now and check in with him. We have backup out there and these nifty next-century watches that do everything but wash the car. If I can't call later and things are going to shit, I can just press the warning button, and he'll come barreling in."

"Let's hope it doesn't come to that."

Si picked up on the first ring, as if he'd been sitting there with the phone in his hand.

"Go ahead," he said.

Max dove right into what he wanted to know.

"I'd tell you to stay alert," Si told him, "but you're

the master of that. George, Kevin, and two others of my men met up with Lou Valenti last night. They're staged at a piece of property about ten miles from Whitlow's lodge. That was as close as they could get."

"I'm surprised they got that close," Max commented. "Whitlow's property has to be more than a hundred acres, which is about average for around here. But I checked it out when we drove here, and there didn't seem to be any vacant properties."

"One of the reasons why Lou is such an asset. The property just west of Whitlow's is owned by people who also only show up a few times a year. They've asked Lou to keep an eye on it."

Today, she wore slacks, so she tucked her gun at the small of her back. Her casual jacket was loose and covered it well. Max did the same, choosing to wear a loose, tight-weave soft-collared shirt that would conceal the weapon. They checked that they had their secure cell phones and their special pens with them. Then they grabbed their folders from the day before.

"Well, Mrs. Ferren," Max said just before he opened their door, "I guess we're all set. Let's just be ready for anything. I hope we at least get the name of who the face of this would be if they succeeded."

"Me, too. But they won't succeed, Max. We're

going to stop them."

*****

Breakfast was over and the dishes cleared, and everyone was back at their seats at the table with full coffee mugs. They had their folders open and pens out, and Max made sure he and Regan had their special pens in their hands.

"Okay." Jed Whitlow looked around. "We have the shipments confirmed, the cartel soldiers at the ready, a schedule for when each event is to take place."

"I have a question." Lorena looked at Max. "Did you happen to bring any of the weapons you'll be shipping so we can take a look at them? Maybe you could give us a demonstration."

"I don't think that's necessary," Jed told her. "We won't be firing the weapons ourselves."

"Luis wants to be absolutely sure they'll be top quality. He doesn't want inferior goods that will derail the entire event."

Max looked at Lorena. He and Si had discussed this, but neither of them was excited about the prospect of doing this.

"You can rest assured only the finest weapons are being loaded for the shipments." He looked over at Jed. "You saw them when you visited the factory, right?"

"I did. I even test fired a couple myself. Tell Luis to put a cork in it, Lorena. It's all good. Now." He opened his folder. "Today we need to review the outline for what takes place afterward."

"I believe we're using your helicopter to get to D.C., Gavin?" He looked at Gavin Emery.

"Yes. We avoid airports that way, and I have just the place to land. The SUVs will be waiting for us."

"Five of them?" Lorena asked.

Gavin nodded. "One for each of us. I contracted with Downrange Security, as we discussed. Three guards for each of us, fully armed. They've been paid and the men will be there waiting for us. They're also providing the SUVs."

"The city will be in chaos after the explosions and killings on the National Mall," Jed continued. "We'll go directly to the White House. Our man will be there waiting for us. The president and his family are scheduled to be at the Washington Mall and, if they are not dead, they will have been hustled off somewhere by the Secret Service. We—"

"What about the vice president?" Elizabeth Emery asked. "Is that taken care of, also?"

"Yes." Jed looked around the table. "As we

discussed, Luis's men will handle that during the explosions."

Listening to the litany, Max had a hard time controlling both his nausea and his anger. These people were discussing the murder of both the president and vice president of the United States as if it was just another activity. He curled his fingers around his pen so hard he was afraid he'd break it and ruin the information it had gathered. If Regan hadn't filtered out the bits and pieces of conversation, beginning with the transport and smuggling into the country of high-value terrorist threats, July 4th would end up being the most disastrous day for this country yet.

"Newsom will be waiting for us at the White House," Jed continued. "He's been briefed and is more than ready to step forward."

Max worked hard to conceal his shock. *Grant Newsom*? The Speaker of the House? The man who couldn't control his own party in the House? *This* was the man chosen to lead the country back from disaster? Holy fucking god!

Whitlow looked at Kurt Cavanaugh. "He knows he's just the figurehead, right?"

Cavanaugh nodded. "That's really all he wants.

Leading the House is a job that's way beyond his skillset, but he loves the publicity, the parties, and the media appearances. When we get to the White House, I'll go to him directly. I've sent him the prepared statement, and I promise he'll be ready for the media. I also sent him his speech to the House of Representatives. Whoever survives, that is."

Max was afraid to even glance sideways at Regan. They had to get this information to Si ASAP. No doubt about it. And what was up with Anna Whitlow, pulling her cell phone out of her pocket every ten minutes to look at the screen.

"Max?" He realized Jed was speaking to him.

"Sorry. I was just taking it all in. Bernardo briefed me but listening to it here makes it all real."

"Oh, it's real all right." Jed grinned. "Three weeks from now, we'll be in charge of it all."

"Bernardo didn't get into this," he said, "but how long do you predict it will take before the smoke dies down—no pun intended—and we have everything under control? And is there an immediate meeting planned so we can coordinate everything?"

"Yes." Elizabeth Emery was the one who answered. "We'll be meeting in the White House. Our security details will be with us in case there are any problems."

"What about the Secret Service?" Regan asked. "Won't we be using them?"

Jed shook his head. "No. We're disbanding them and using our own people. More control that way."

"Sounds good."

Sounds insane! He had to get this to Si. He couldn't wait until later. However, he forced himself to sit there until it got to be noon and Jed called a halt for lunch.

"I'll be back down in a minute," he said as he rose from his seat. "There are some things I need that I left in my room. More information about the guns and ammo that I wanted to pass around."

Before anyone could say a word, he was heading upstairs, forcing himself to walk slowly although he wanted to take them two at a time. He hustled into the bathroom, turned on the faucet, and called Si.

"Go," Si said when he answered the phone.

"You are. Not fucking going to believe this," Max said, then laid everything out for the man.

"Holy goddamn shit. Are you kidding me?"

"Not even a little. Si, we have to stop this."

"No shit." Silence filled the air. "Okay, we need to get the two of you out of there. Now."

“But there may be more they’re planning to discuss this afternoon,” Max protested.

“I don’t care if they want to talk all goddamn night. There’s still the chance that Luis Rojas’s visit could have provided them with more information than we know. It at least has made them sit on the edge of their chairs. Let me get it set up and I’ll text you.”

“What about just coming in here and arresting them?”

“Not until I have this all tied up so tight there’s no way for them to find a way out. And I need to make sure nothing leaves the Ferren factory, but I don’t want to tip my hand yet. We’ve got a little wiggle room there.”

“What do you want me to do?”

“I want you to go back downstairs and have lunch and talk to these people and try not to shoot them while I work things out on this end. Watch for my text.”

“Max?” A knock on the door and Regan calling to him.

“Coming.” He opened the door and pulled her into the bathroom. “I wish I had time to give you a proper kiss and wash away the bad taste in my mouth.”

“No kidding. Did you get hold of Si? I figured

that's what you were doing."

"Yes. He wants us out of here ASAP."

"But—"

"But nothing. He says it's too dangerous for us to stay here now. He's getting our exfil ready and will text me." He gave her a quick, hard hug.

"He's the boss. Come on. Let's go try and eat lunch and see what the afternoon brings."

The afternoon brought more of the same with one exception. Everyone at the table seemed a lot more uptight, and every so often he would catch someone glancing at both him and Regan with a strange look. He was beginning to think Si was right and they needed to split ASAP.

Nothing changed until late in the afternoon when there was a knock on the door.

"I'll get it," Lorena said, pushing her chair back.

Everyone seemed to freeze in their seats while she walked to the entrance. Max watched her carefully, shocked to see Luis Rojas and three men who could only be his "fixers" walk into the room. The muscles in his stomach tightened, and he pushed back in his chair, reaching slowly for his gun. Before he could get his hand around the grip, Gavin Emery was behind hm, grabbing his wrist. When he glanced at Regan, he saw Whitlow had pulled her from her chair and yanked her hands behind her back. In seconds, he had her gun, also.

"What the hell is going on here?" he demanded.

Anna Whitlow looked up at him from her place at the table.

"I had a very short but interesting phone call while you and Regan were upstairs," she told him. "I remembered that I had the number for Jeanne Ferren's very private cell phone, so I tried to call her. You know. Just to verify that the two of you were the real deal. I waited all day for her to get back to me. If she was really in the hospital sitting with her husband, she would have called me back right away. But finally she did."

Oh shit.

"And what did she say?"

"She had a very interesting story to tell me, but I'm sure you know all the details. About Bernardo's fake heart attack, the threats from the government. She said as soon as Jed had visited Bernardo in the hospital and gone home, they moved her and Bernardo to a house somewhere with deathly frightening men to guard them, no telephones or other means of communication. She was lucky she'd had the presence of mind to hide the one cell. They've got her and Bernardo locked away there, while the real Max and Regan are under guard somewhere else."

Max stood silently taking it all in. Waiting for whatever came next.

"Nothing to say?" Jed asked.

Max wondered why the fuck her guards hadn't confiscated her cell phone, but Anna's next words answered his question.

"Before they let the Ferrens pack their things, they took their cell phones, laptops, any other electronics. But clever Jeanne had this other cell that she managed to wrap in her panties when she packed, but she wasn't alone long enough to make a call until today."

"You think we're idiots, Max?" Lorena sneered. "Or whatever your name is. We didn't trust you from the beginning. Luis took a little trip to scope things out that really set us to thinking."

"So, I reached out to Jeanne," Anne put in. "As I said, it took all day, but she finally called back."

Max looked around at everyone. "You'll never get away with this. Just so you know."

Jed glared at him. "We've put too much into this to let you ruin it. Our plan will still go forward."

"Yeah? Exactly how will you do that?" He looked

at Rojas. "And what the fuck are you doing here?"

"Luis is going to take your lady on a little trip, where she'll be comfortable until the Fourth of July. After that, it won't matter."

After that, we'll both be dead, he thought.

"And what about me? There are people waiting to hear from me."

The smile on Whitlow's face was anything but warm. "You will be our guest until the Fourth of July. When we leave here, tomorrow you'll come to my ranch with me, where you'll be my guest for the next couple of weeks. When we've taken over the country, we'll let you go."

Yeah, right.

He took a step toward Regan, where one of Luis's goons was holding her, clutching her arms. Whitlow pulled him back. He could have broken the hold, but the circumstances at the moment weren't favorable for any kind of success here.

Whitlow stripped both of them of weapons and set them on the table.

"I'll just take these while I'm at it," Whitlow said. "You won't be using them."

Max stood there, grinding his teeth. At the moment, the odds were stacked against him. He might be a SEAL but he wasn't Superman. He needed to make a plan, and that involved getting up to his room and retrieving his other cell phone.

"Don't try anything," Whitlow added. "We'd have to kill you both right here, and that would really mess up this room."

Max's mind was working overtime. He sent Regan a silent message to do what they said. None of them were aware of two important things: he and Regan wore watches with GPS locators in them, and Si's people were not far from this place.

I'll be fine, she mouthed at him, but it didn't make him feel any better.

"You're making a big mistake." He spoke to the room at large. "You have no idea whom you're up against."

"No, you're the one who has no idea," Lorena told him. "You and whoever you work for must think we're all a bunch of dunces. You'll find out you're not dealing with powerless idiots."

He wanted to say they were the ones in for a surprise, but he didn't. He stood there, blocked by Whitlow and Emery, while Rojas and his thugs took Regan out the door. If they harmed so much as one hair on her head, he'd find each of them and make sure they died a slow and very painful death.

The men holding him back finally released him. The front door opened again, and two men who looked like they were employees of Thugs-R-Us walked in.

"Part of my security team," Whitlow told him. "Hank will be sitting right outside your door, just in case you thought you might take a walk. Make yourself comfortable. Someone will bring dinner up to you later."

When Hank grabbed his arm with thick fingers, he yanked it free.

"No touching," he said. "I can walk by myself."

"Okay. Just don't try any funny stuff."

Max had no intention of it. He had a plan, and he didn't want to call any undue attention to himself right now.

When they reached his room, Hank couldn't stop himself from giving Max a shove. Max didn't even stumble, just walked into the room and waited while Hank stepped out into the hall and closed the door. He waited two minutes to make sure the hulk wasn't about to pop back into the room. Then he went into the bathroom, closed and locked the door—at least this door *had* a lock—and fished the two phones out from under the sink. He activated them both then put one in his pants pocket.

Instead of calling Si, since his voice just might be heard, he typed a message.

Cover blown. Rojas has Regan. Activate GPS trace.

He waited nearly a full minute before an answer came back.

Done. Called Kevin to watch for it on his laptop. They will find car.

Approach carefully.

What am I, an idiot?

Max actually grinned.

Going to try leaving. Have a way. Will contact you in a few.

Let me know. Kevin can jam outgoing signals from the lodge.

K.

Next, he grabbed the suitcase from the closet and opened the concealed compartment. There was a third handgun in there, a Glock 42, what was known as a pocket pistol. He shoved it along with three extra clips of ammo into his pockets and replaced the suitcase.

He'd done some recon when they first got here in case a situation just like this came up. There was a huge tree with thick branches right outside their bedroom window, part of a small stand at that side of the house. He hadn't done anything like this for a while, and his shoulder was still questionable, but he really didn't have a choice.

He eased the window open and removed the screen, which came out easily. Getting himself out and onto the thick branch that nearly touched the side of the house wasn't as bad as he thought. He was even, thankfully, able to lean over, lower the window, and replace the screen. The great room had no visuals on this side of the house, so there was no one to notice what was happening.

He made his way down the tree, gritting his teeth against the stress on his shoulder. Once on the ground, he blended into the thicket and made his way to the open land beyond it. He just had to get to the forested area on the other side of it, and he'd be good. He ran faster than he ever had in his life, not even bothering to look over his shoulder. If someone spotted him, he'd hear the sound of their bullets.

At last he was in the trees again, and he pulled out his cell, punching in Si's number.

"I'm out," he said.

Si grunted. "Of course you are. I never had a doubt. I'm activating the GPS locator for your signal."

Max continued to make his way through the trees toward the highway while he waited for Si.

"Okay. All set. I called Kevin and told them to pick you up. They're only five minutes away by car."

"Then we get Regan."

"Yes, sailor. Then we get Regan."

He had just made it to the road when a black sedan headed toward him. He ducked down behind the trees until it pulled to the shoulder and stopped.

"I've got you, Max," Kevin called out. "Get in so we can get the fuck out of here and retrieve Regan, or Si will skin all of us."

Max heaved himself into the back seat of the car and George, who was driving, took off like a bat out of hell.

Chapter Thirteen

"I suppose someone should check on Max Whatever His Last Name is," Anna said.

"Why?" Jed asked. "He isn't going anywhere."

"True. I just thought we might get him down here and find out who he works for. Who got onto us and how."

Lorena gave an unladylike snort. "You think he'd tell you? I'd bet he's former military and has withstood more than you can dish out to him."

"You haven't seen me at work," Gavin told her.

She actually burst out laughing. "Gavin, you're a fifty-five-year-old rancher who has never been in the military yourself. Wrestling bulls isn't the same thing."

"So, you don't think we should try to question him?"

"I don't think we'll get anything from him, but you're certainly welcome to try."

Gavin looked around the table. "What do you all think?"

Elizabeth, his wife, leaned forward. "I think I'd like to know where whoever planted them found someone who could be a double for the real Max Ferren."

"And I'd like to know more about where Jeanne and Bernardo are," Anna added.

"Fine," Jed said. "Then let's get him down here." He went to the foot of the stairs. "Hank, let's get Max Whoever down here and have a chat with him."

Hank stood up from the chair he'd been sitting in, knocked on the bedroom door, opened it, and walked in. He was back out in five seconds.

"He's gone."

Jed stared up at him. "What do you mean, he's gone? Where the hell did he go?"

"I don't know, sir."

Jed was already taking the stairs two at a time, and he sensed others behind him. He followed Hank into the room which, true enough, was empty. They even checked under the beds and in the closet, but there wasn't a sign of him anywhere. Jed walked over to the window that looked out onto the little grove of trees, but the window was closed and the screen neatly in place.

"I'll be fucked," he said in a soft voice.

"You very well may be," Lorena agreed. "Did he vaporize and disappear into thin air? Maybe through the air-conditioning vent?"

"Don't be ridiculous," he snapped.

"Then tell me how he did it. And even more importantly, where the hell is he?"

Everyone had crowded into the room by this time, and they were all demanding answers. Jed wanted to tell them to shut the fuck up.

"This all started with your friend," Kurt Cavanaugh pointed out. "Your friend and his fake heart attack."

"It looked damn real to me when I went to see him," Jed snapped.

"Well, somehow someone got to him," Lorena pointed out. "And everything went to hell after that."

"Maybe someone else should have checked out the hospital," Gavin growled.

"And you would have seen exactly what I did," Jed snapped, "Which was what they wanted. What they staged."

"We aren't doing any good clustered in this bedroom," Lorena said. "Let's go downstairs and gather ourselves together. We need to call Luis and make sure he has Regan or whatever her name is hidden away, and that his men are ready for the big day. Check that everything is still a go at the factory.

But for god's sake, don't say a word to Newsome about this. He'll shit his pants."

In seconds, they were all back in their seats at the table, and Lorena had picked up her cell to dial Luis.

"Put it on speaker," Jed told her, "so we can all hear."

She shot him a nasty look but did so. But when she dialed the number, instead of a ringtone, they got what sounded like a fast busy signal. She frowned, looked at the phone, frowned some more, and redialed, with the same results.

"Let me try it," Gavin said. "Give me the number."

Lorena recited it to him. He dialed and got exactly the same result.

"Damn it to hell, anyway." He slammed his phone down. "Someone's jamming the signal from this building."

His wife stared at him. "Is that possible? And who would be doing it?"

"The fucking government," Gavin said. "That's who."

"And that's where our so-called guests came from." Jed slammed his fist on the table. "Damn it to hell."

There was silence around the table. Then Lorena

sat back in her chair.

"We'd better figure out what to do pretty damn quick, or this whole thing will fall apart."

"If it hasn't already," Jed muttered under his breath.

*****.

The car dumped Max, Kevin, and George out where the helo had landed, a big, dark-green machine whose rotors were still spinning lazily. A man Max didn't recognize, dressed in fatigues, stood beside it.

"That GPS signal is about two miles down this road," he told them. "Get your asses in here."

They climbed in, Kevin carrying his laptop with all the programs on it, and, in seconds, they were in the air. Max took out his pocket pistol, but George just laughed.

"That won't even frighten my kid," he said. He reached into the back and pulled out two Glocks plus an AR-15, offering Max his choice.

"A Glock." He took it and checked the magazine, cocked the slide. "I'm ready."

"Good," George told him. "I like this other one better."

"There's the car," Kevin said and turned to the pilot. "Can we set down in front of it?"

"Sure, as long as he doesn't run into me and ruin my machine."

"Make it happen."

They flew low over the speeding car, turned around ahead of it, and hovered in the road. Max could see a window lowered, and a hand with a gun poked out.

"Oh, he doesn't want to do that," Max said in a dark voice.

He slid the window in the chopper down just enough, stuck his hand out, and fired six shots from the Glock in rapid succession. With his usual precision, he hit the shooter's hand, and the gun dropped to the highway. The chopper hovered just above the ground, in place, low enough that Max and Kevin could both jump out and begin shooting at the car again, hitting all four tires. With no place to go, the driver screeched to a halt.

A door opened, and Luis slid out, dragging Regan with him. Max noted that she looked slightly disheveled but otherwise unharmed.

"If you want your woman back," he shouted at Max, "drop the guns, take me in the helicopter to wherever I tell you, and I will let her go."

He shook his head. "Not today." He lifted his gun.

"Do it, Regan." He just hoped she was military enough to get his signal.

At once, she stepped on Luis's foot and bent over. Max sighted, fired, and the bullet entered the center of Luis's forehead. The man collapsed to the ground, nearly taking Regan with him, but Max rushed forward and grabbed her. He handed his gun to Kevin and pulled Regan close against his chest, arms around her, brushing kisses on her forehead and smoothing her hair.

"I'm okay," she told him in a shaky voice, "but can we go home now?"

He chuckled. "My thoughts exactly."

Epilogue

They lay in the very big bed, naked and sated, drinking the last of the champagne and watching television. The last three weeks had been grueling. Max and Regan had met extensively with Si and his bosses. Their pens had picked up enough audio and video to put what Regan called the unholy group away for three lifetimes. They would go on trial for a number of crimes, not the least of which was treason.

Si had sent teams to each of their homes to gather every paper that could be found, any records at all, although the evidence from the meeting at Whitlow's lodge would be more than enough. Ferren Arms and Munitions had been closed down and all their inventory confiscated by DHS. It would take a long time to put all the evidence in order, but government attorneys were already working on it.

Grant Newsome had been arrested at his home in Washington. Si had run two scenarios past his boss, and they had decided to go with the one Si and Max both wanted—full on, with media onsite to capture it. DHS had put together a team, men in suits plus those in battle gear and fully armed. Si himself had led the group, knocking on Newsome's door at six in the morning.

Max and Regan, for their work, had been allowed to observe from a big black SUV with tinted windows. Regan said she'd never forget the sight of Newsome in his pajamas and bathrobe opening the door to what awaited him, taking one look, and passing out.

The cabal had all been arraigned, another field day for the press. DHS, with the president's approval, wanted to send a message loud and clear to anyone who thought they could attack the United States from the inside and take control. The next few months, or however long it took to bring them all to trial, would be given over to the teams of attorneys. By the time it was all finished, there wouldn't be enough left of the fortunes they had amassed to buy a good hamburger.

The death of Luis Rojas left the doors wide open on his cartel. The last Si had learned, there was much infighting and bloodshed to see who would take over.

"Good riddance," he told them.

They all knew another leader would rise, but by then the cartel would have been broken up into smaller groups, its power diluted.

When the Fourth of July rolled around, Max and

Regan, still in D. C., had decided they'd spend the day watching celebrations on television. The president, believing they should honor as many of them as possible, had convinced the networks to do cut-ins from celebrations all over the country. Max and Regan had spent the day in bed, watching them, drinking champagne, and having incredible sex.

"They don't know how close so many of them came to being blown up," Regan murmured.

"No, they don't. And let's hope they never do."

Max placed his champagne glass on the nightstand, took Regan's, and put it down beside his. Then he rolled her naked body against his and gave her a kiss so slow and sweet yet hot and sexy, he discovered that even after the many times they'd already made love, he was again unbelievably hard.

"You might be dangerous to my health," he teased.

Her laugh was slow and sexy. "But what a way to go, right?"

He continued stroking her arm lazily. "Ever been to Maine?"

"Hmm. Maine? Can't say that I have. Why? What's up there for me?"

"Well, the Atlantic Ocean. A typical small Maine town. A beat-up former SEAL who's finally ready to settle down. Now that he's found the woman of his heart, that is."

She looked at him. "And have you? Found the woman of your heart?"

He nodded. "I just hope she's on the same page I am."

"And what page is that?"

"I'm in love with you, Regan. I know it's been fast, and under difficult circumstances. But I knew it the moment we met. You're everything I've been looking for all my life." He tilted her face up so he could look in her eyes. "Tell me how you feel."

"Truth? I never thought I'd find love again after Dylan. Then I met you, and you turned my world upside down. So yes. I'd love to go to Maine with you and see about a life together."

He hadn't realized how tense he was until she said the words. Then he relaxed, and his lips turned up in a wide grin.

"Good. We'll leave first thing in the morning." He rolled them so he was between her thighs and grinned at her. "I have big plans for tonight."

Silver SEALs

Did you enjoy this story? Read through the other stories in the Sleeper SEALs Series by eleven other fantastic military romance authors:

Make sure to pick up ALL the books in the Sleeper SEAL series. These can be read in any order and each stands alone.

#1 Cat Johns SEAL Strong

#2 Sharon Hamilton SEAL Love's Legacy

#3 Maryann Jordan SEAL Together

#4 Donna Michaels SEAL in Charge

#5 Kalyn Cooper SEAL in a Storm

#6 Kris Michaels SEAL Forever

#7 Abbie Zanders SEAL Out of Water

#8 Geri Foster SEAL and Deliver

#9 J. M. Madden SEAL Hard

#10 Desiree Holt SEAL Undercover

#11 Trish Loye SEAL Forever

#12 Caitlyn O'Leary SEAL at Sunrise